"Born in a gypsy caravan in Romania," *she began.*

"Sold to an Irish tavern owner who thought I could dance. Then a Greek shipping tycoon offered me a job as target for the knife thrower in his circus. Later, I ended up on a Mississippi riverboat, where a gambler taught me how to cheat at cards . . . and that's how I made my fortune!" Raven finished lightly.

Josh burst out laughing.

Raven gave her imagination a rest for a moment and politely asked, "And how was your life to date?"

"Oh, dull, compared to yours," he told her.

"You mean, after I bared my soul, you're not going to share the details?"

"I'm trying to entice you with my mystery," he explained gravely.

"It's not working," she said.

"Well, you seem to be above bribery. I offered you my kingdom and you weren't impressed. And last night when I was drunk you removed half my clothes, but my bare and manly chest seems not to have inspired one pang of lust. Then when I paraded before you clad only in a towel, you didn't even blink."

Raven choked on her laughter.

"I see I haven't been going about this the right way." Purposely Josh rose from his chair and lifted her to her feet. "Clearly, what is needed here," he said firmly, "is a little old-fashioned persuasion." And he bent his dark head to hers . . .

WHAT ARE *LOVESWEPT* ROMANCES?

They are stories of true romance and touching emotion. We believe those two very important ingredients are constants in our highly sensual and very believable stories in the *LOVESWEPT* line. Our goal is to give you, the reader, stories of consistently high quality that may sometimes make you laugh, sometimes make you cry, but are always fresh and creative and contain many delightful surprises within their pages.

Most romance fans read an enormous number of books. Those they truly love, they keep. Others may be traded with friends and soon forgotten. We hope that each *LOVESWEPT* romance will be a treasure—a "keeper." We will always try to publish

LOVE STORIES YOU'LL NEVER FORGET
BY AUTHORS YOU'LL ALWAYS REMEMBER

The Editors

LOVESWEPT® · 193

Kay Hooper
Raven on the Wing

BANTAM BOOKS
TORONTO · NEW YORK · LONDON · SYDNEY · AUCKLAND

RAVEN ON THE WING
A Bantam Book / May 1987

If you would be interested in receiving protective vinyl
covers for your Loveswept books, please write to this address
for information:

Loveswept
Bantam Books, Inc.
P.O. Box 985
Hicksville, NY 11802

ISBN 0-553-21824-7

Published simultaneously in the United States and Canada

Bantam Books are published by Bantam Books, Inc. Its trademark, consisting of the words "Bantam Books" and the por-
trayal of a rooster, is Registered in U.S. Patent and Trademark
Office and in other countries. Marca Registrada. Bantam
Books, Inc., 666 Fifth Avenue, New York, New York 10103.

PRINTED IN THE UNITED STATES OF AMERICA

O   0 9 8 7 6 5 4 3 2 1

One

The party was lousy, Josh thought as he made his way to the door. He would have thanked his hostess, except that he had no idea who she was. He was in Los Angeles on a whistle-stop tour of some of his businesses—a hotel here—and had been invited to this party by a man interested in buying into the hotel business. Josh had been bored, and the party had sounded better than any other activity he could think of.

It hadn't been, however. And his distaste had increased an hour before when Leon Travers had arrived to be welcomed servilely by the evening's host; Josh could think of numerous ways for a businessman to advance himself, but selling his soul to the devil was not on the list. His host, it seemed, thought otherwise; he obviously believed the sun rose behind Leon Travers's silver head.

Josh could have disabused him of that idea, but knew only too well that people had to make their own mistakes.

Now, as he made his way through the crush of glittering people, he felt definitely jaded. He was supposed to leave Los Angeles tomorrow, and he found no regret in putting this city behind him. But no longing for the next city, either, and no longing for home.

Home. He owned four homes. A penthouse condo in New York, a ranch in Montana, a vacation lodge in the Catskills, and a lonely cliff-hugging aerie on the coast of Oregon. None of them held any appeal for him at the moment.

He found his coat with some difficulty, then squeezed his way out the front door of the hotel suite. For a moment, he stood in the hallway, allowing his ears to adjust to the relative silence. Then he strode down the hall. Occupied with dark thoughts, he only dimly heard the muffled bell of the elevator around the corner. Walking briskly to catch it, he was abruptly hit by something warm and soft, yet with a force that knocked him backward to measure his length on the carpeted floor. The fall jarred him, but it was when he looked up at his attacker that he lost his breath.

In a flashing instant, what he saw sparked a double reaction within him. His body throbbed strongly, searingly, in an instantaneous arousal; never in his life had he felt such desire so quickly or powerfully. And deep inside him, another response to what he saw caused his heart to turn over with an almost-painful lurch. He thought of all those years of caution and avoidance guided by his conviction that he had only to keep his hand firmly on the wheel of his ship and his eyes away from brunettes to control his destiny.

While his heart and body grappled with powerful new feelings, Josh could regard the situation only with ironic amusement. How else could a reasonably intelligent man react to the knowledge that the fates were probably laughing themselves silly?

"Oh, hell," he muttered despairingly. "I knew it. I knew you were out there somewhere. And I was so *careful*."

She wasn't listening.

"Ye gods and little fishes! The saleslady *said* this dress would knock men flat, but I don't think this is what she meant. Damn, and I'll bet you broke something too! Listen, I don't believe it's ethical to sue one's fellow humans. And in this case it'd hardly be *fair* because we were both moving. I mean, it isn't as if my car hit yours when it was parked. Right?"

He raised himself on his elbows, crossed his ankles, and stared up at her in utter fascination.

She was tall, he judged, and blessed by the Creator with a body that could—and most likely did—stop traffic; it was certainly stopping his heart about every third beat. She seemed in imminent danger of escaping from the blue silk dress she wore, yet there wasn't an ounce of excess flesh on her slender frame. Full breasts, narrow waist, curved hips.

Unconsciously, he swallowed hard.

Her long legs were not only eye-catching, he decided wistfully, but painted vivid images in his mind of strong silken thighs wrapped around him. . . . He swallowed hard again and gazed at the crowning glory that had so swiftly and completely blasted his so-called control into pieces.

Impossibly blue-black hair swung free and beautiful to the small of her back.

Her face was not beautiful, but having seen it once, no one would ever forget it. She was striking. Elegant. Wide, merry violet eyes, an aristocratic nose, and lips curved with laughter were the features that would always be remembered.

And Josh, never one to waste time, sighed and abandoned himself to fate. "I'm Joshua Long," he said. "Marry me."

"Oh, you hit your head when you fell, didn't you? Here, let me help you up."

He accepted the offered hand and climbed to his feet, never taking his eyes from her elegant face. "What's your name?" he asked, holding on to her slender hand and amazingly conscious of the contact.

"Raven," she answered, her voice soothing. "Horrible, isn't it? Were you leaving? I'll get you a cab; you shouldn't drive in your condition."

"Raven." He was delighted. Her eyes were incredible. He hadn't seen eyes like that since—he'd *never* seen eyes like that. "Marry me, Raven."

"Oh, damn, I *know* I'm going to get sued!" She moaned, allowing him to continue to hold her hand as she led him gently toward the elevator. "Maybe I should take you to the emergency room."

"I didn't hit my head," he murmured as they stood in the elevator. Then, suddenly panicked, he lifted the hand he was holding—her left—and stared at it. Panic faded, along with the dizzying rush of peculiar savagery he'd abruptly felt. "You aren't married? Engaged?"

"What's taking this damn thing so long?" she asked, stabbing at a button with one finger. "No,

I'm not married. Or engaged. D'you have a doctor? Should I take you to your doctor?"

"Have a drink with me instead," he countered. Then, reflecting, he added, "Or I'll sue."

"There's a tavern around the corner," she said hastily. "We can walk. Can you make it that far?"

"Just don't let go of me," he answered deviously.

"No, I won't do that," she promised, leading him from the elevator and across the lobby.

It was a good thing she didn't let go of him, Josh thought as they made their way along the lighted sidewalk. He paid no attention at all to where they were going, but instead gazed at her profile. He no longer felt jaded. In fact, he'd never in his life felt so captivated. Everything about her, every quality, every word, charmed him completely.

And since he was a grown man with at least some control over the urges of his body, he managed not to lunge at her. Barely. But the instant throbbing he'd felt upon looking up at her had not lessened; he could feel that slow, constant pulse of desire more vividly than ever before in his life. His body felt heated, abnormally sensitive; all his consciousness seemed focused on her with an intensity that left room for nothing else.

She led him through the door of a small tavern and into the dark, smoky interior, waving her free hand at the huge, burly bartender. "Hi, Jake!"

"Raven! What can I get for you, kid?"

She glanced at Josh, then looked back at Jake. "Brandy. Two of them. We'll be in a booth."

"Right," he called back.

Raven led Josh to a booth, waving cheerfully at a few of the other patrons in the crowded bar, but being careful never to lose her grip on his hand.

When they were seated, she attempted gently to reclaim her hand. Josh held on.

"I think you're going to need both hands for your glass," she told him patiently.

"I didn't hit my head, you know," he remarked idly, staring at her. He couldn't stop staring at her. "Raven what?"

"Isn't that an insane name? I told Pop when I was ten that he shouldn't have let Mother get away with it. But he said he'd felt guilty because he had all the fun and she did all the work. So he feels guilty and I get stuck with the name of a bird and a long, rambling poem."

" 'Once upon a midnight dreary,' " Josh remembered.

She shuddered. "Right. D'you know how many times I've heard that poem in my life? Every guy I ever went out with memorized the damn thing. You obviously know it. Don't recite it. Please."

"All right," he said equably; he wanted to please her and would have quite literally done anything she asked. "Are you hungry? Do they serve food here?"

"I've eaten, thanks. But—" She looked up as Jake materialized at their booth holding brandy. "Jake, could we have some chips or something?"

"Sure. Another stray, Raven?"

Josh looked at him. "She's going to marry me."

The bartender looked at Raven. "Is he serious?"

"I knocked him down," she explained. "I think he hit his head."

"I'll get the chips," Jake said, and vanished.

"Drink your brandy," Raven told Josh firmly. "You need it."

After a swallow of the fiery liquid, Josh found

his thoughts focusing on the situation. "Why won't you marry me?" he demanded fiercely. "I'm perfectly all right, and I have pots of money."

"Just like a leprechaun," she murmured.

"That's pots of *gold*," he corrected her. "I have cold hard cash. And businesses and things. Hotels. Property. Marry me."

Clearly, she was intrigued; he could tell from the way she looked at him.

"Listen, do the authorities know you've escaped? I mean, normally I'd be too polite to ask, but if there's a reward or something, I wouldn't mind collecting it."

"I'm not crazy," he assured her, but silently amended the thought. He didn't *think* he was crazy.

"Of course not," she agreed sympathetically. She looked at his glass. "Maybe brandy wasn't such a good idea."

"Marry me," he said.

She sighed and spoke in the soothing tone of one humoring a rather sweet lunatic. "Gee, I'd really like to, but I have to get my hair done."

"Waste of money," he said. "It's beautiful."

"Thank you." She was polite, clearly not flattered. "Should I call someone for you? Someone who might worry that you're loo—uh, missing?"

"Don't you believe in love at first sight?" he asked anxiously.

She gazed at him, the merry violet eyes rueful. "It sounds just lovely," she said. "So do fairy tales. Look, mister—"

"Josh."

"Josh, if you're looking for a teeth-rattling night, cruise the bars. I'm not interested in a fling."

"I'm not interested in a fling either," he told her patiently. "I want to marry you."

"You don't know me."

"I," he said, "believe in love at first sight. Now." He studied her elegant, polite face, then sighed as Jake returned with a basket of chips. "She won't marry me," he told the other man.

Jake looked fiercely at Raven. "Why won't you marry him, Raven?"

"Go back to the bar, Jake."

He grinned and winked at her. "Just thought I'd ask." Then he turned and walked back toward the crowded bar.

Josh yelled after him to bring two more brandies. He had a vague idea of getting her drunk just so he could propose, she could—would? maybe—say yes, and he could hold her to her word tomorrow.

After finishing her third brandy, matching him easily, she leaned toward him conspiratorially over the hand he was still holding, and said, "It won't work, you know."

"What?" he asked.

"Trying to get me drunk. I could put you under this table. I could put you, everyone in this bar, and the Russian *Army* under the table. Drinking straight vodka. On an empty stomach."

Josh possessed a hard head and a cast-iron stomach. Most of the time, anyway. He wasn't so sure about now. However . . . He had never in his life been falling-down drunk. So he was confident. Overly confident.

He yelled for more brandy.

· · ·

Even before he opened his eyes, Josh remembered the night before. Sort of. He remembered very clearly asking Raven if he could drink champagne from her shoe, and he remembered her reply that open-toed sandals weren't too good for such a thing. He remembered challenging another patron of the bar to an arm-wrestling contest; in retrospect, he decided that had been dumb. His arm felt dead except for the pain in his fingernails.

He remembered telling a long and somewhat involved story to anyone and everyone who would listen, including a wooden Indian standing in a corner. He remembered chasing Raven around a table. Or three. He remembered solemnly offering her four homes, six Learjets, the Hope diamond, southern Montana, a mink coat, a Porsche, and the rest of his drink if she'd only marry him. He remembered she'd laughed.

She'd laughed a lot.

After that, things got *really* hazy.

He tried to open his eyes. Some idiot, he discovered, had sandpapered the lids. And another idiot had hung the sun right in front of him; it was hellishly bright. He closed his eyes and tried to groan, discovering that sound had a disastrous effect on his head; little men with sledgehammers were building a skyscraper in there. He bit back a second groan, fearing the skyscraper would collapse and squash his brain.

A pleasing herbal scent wafted to him.

"Can you sit up?"

His lids snapped up, and raw eyes moved to locate her, finally, standing by the bed. In spite of his body's abused condition, the throb of desire was instant and sent a shaft of exquisite agony all the way to the top of his head. He didn't mind the pain. She was wearing jeans and a bulky knit sweater, and he fell in love all over again. Being in love, he wanted to please her. Except—

"My left arm's dead," he managed to croak.

"I'm not surprised." Her voice was very soft; clearly, she knew the condition of his head. "You arm-wrestled a man who looked like the starting lineup of a pro football team. All by himself."

With a tremendous effort and more than a little help from her, Josh managed to sit up. He told himself fiercely he was hardly in any condition to ravish brunettes, and so was able—barely—to control urges leaping through him at the first touch of her helping hand. Pillows were banked behind him while he discovered he was wearing only his trousers. He indulged briefly in a rush of heated images in which Raven undressed him, then pushed the thoughts away; in that direction, he decided, lay madness.

He was in a soft bed in a bright, cheerful bedroom, and it was sometime the next day.

She handed him a cup of herbal-smelling brew and sat gingerly on the side of the bed. "Drink that. It'll help."

Somewhat to his surprise, the hot, strong herbal tea did help. His head even began to clear. Suddenly puzzled, he looked down at his numb left arm. "I'm right-handed," he said. "Why on earth did I use my left to wrestle?"

The smile in her merry eyes spread to twitching lips. "Well," she murmured, "you were handicapping yourself. To be fair."

Laughing hurt his head, but Josh didn't mind very much. "Hell," he finally gasped, "I've disgraced

myself and embarrassed you to death, I'm sure."
He was both relieved and disappointed to realize
that he probably hadn't disgraced himself by at-
tacking her; relief won, mainly because that would
have been something he would certainly choose to
remember.

She was still laughing softly. "Not at all. Lots of
my friends have tried to drink me under the table
through the years; I've learned to cope. And you
weren't that bad. You stayed on your feet through
the whole thing."

He thought hard. "I distinctly remember offering you my kingdom if you'd marry me. You
laughed."

"Forgive me," she said solemnly. "But before
that, you'd offered your kingdom for a horse; you
told everyone you wanted to slay dragons for me.
You also bet the kingdom in the arm-wrestling
contest."

"I didn't sign anything, did I?" he asked warily.

"No, but you bought everybody drinks. I finally
took control of your money clip before you could
buy the tavern." She nodded to the nightstand.
"There's quite a bit left, mainly because Jake was
horrified at the way you were throwing money
around and helped me get you into a cab before
you could bankrupt yourself."

He gazed at her elegant face in which warm
violet eyes shone cheerfully, and felt his heart
lurch in the almost-painful manner it had so lately
learned. "If you won't marry me," he said urgently,
"then live with me! I'll convince you to marry me
later."

She blinked. "You know, you slept more than
ten hours, so I have to assume it isn't liquor

talking. And even if that knock on the head gave you a concussion—"

"I didn't hit my head!" he protested.

"—you should be better by now. So either you *aren't* better, or you're mad as a hatter. I don't know whether to call an ambulance or a padded truck."

Josh balanced his cup and saucer on his lap long enough to run a hand through his hair. It struck him somewhat belatedly that he probably looked just dandy for marriage proposals; hung over, bare-chested, morning stubble, and hair flying every which way. Not to mention having clearly convinced her last night that he was either concussed or suffering from lunatic delusions. He tried to think of some way to combat all these deficiencies.

"Raven," he said finally, keeping his voice as level as possible and meeting her eyes steadily, "I am cold sober, not concussed, and perfectly sane. I'm thirty-five years old, which means I generally know my own mind. The moment I saw you, I knew I wanted to marry you. I am not joking about that. I'm not handing you a line.

"I am also aware that you barely know me. My mind tells me that I should, therefore, not expect you to marry me immediately."

She started giggling.

Pained, he stared at her. "All right, I know it sounds arrogant. After knowing me better, you could well decide you'd rather join the Peace Corps or the Foreign Legion."

"Or go into a nunnery," she said, entering into the spirit of things.

He frowned at her. "*Anyway*, what I'm saying is

that I would appreciate it very much if you'd take me seriously."

Raven took his empty cup and rose to her feet. "This tea usually helps a hangover. Why don't you have a hot shower, and I'll fix a late breakfast."

Josh considered food, and found that his stomach didn't reject the idea outright. "Well, but—"

"The bathroom's through there," she said, gesturing toward a doorway. "There's a razor in the top left-hand vanity drawer, and your clothes are on that chair. If you don't want to parade around in a dinner jacket at ten in the morning, check the closet; you might find something to fit. I'll be in the kitchen."

She left.

Moving carefully, Josh took a shower and shaved, then returned to the bedroom to check the closet. What he found sent him immediately to the kitchen of the small apartment wearing nothing but a towel and holding black murder in his heart. Not for her, of course. For the owner of the clothing.

"I hope you have a brother," he announced with what he vaguely realized was inordinate ferocity, waving a handful of clothing at her.

She turned from the stove and stared at him. After a moment, she said dryly, "No, I don't have a brother. I also don't have a lover. This isn't my apartment; it belongs to a friend. The clothes belong to her husband."

"Oh," he said. Black murder gave way to sudden curiosity. He recalled a thought that had occurred to him in the shower. "Where did you sleep?"

"On the couch. Go get dressed."

Josh retreated.

*   *   *

Turning back to the stove, Raven automatically continued preparing breakfast. Looney Tunes, she decided, smiling. The man was obviously Looney Tunes. But he was, at least, an amiable lunatic; other than a fierce glare at his opponent in the infamous arm-wrestling match, he hadn't once lost his temper during the previous evening.

And he'd been flatteringly attentive—except when he'd gotten some story into his head and insisted on telling it to everyone. He'd been indignant when the wooden Indian hadn't laughed.

Raven swallowed a giggle.

No, she decided, all in all the evening had been fun. She didn't even regret missing the party, in spite of whatever consequences might develop. She should, of course, have regretted missing it, and reminded herself of that. There would be questions. A distant, shrewd part of her mind began formulating answers, examining each for flaws.

The rest of her mind concentrated on him. And she wondered what she was going to do with her lunatic. He'd seemed reasonably rational this morning—but then, he'd *sounded* rational last night. Sort of. His voice had been oddly husky whenever he spoke to her, but his tone had been perfectly reasonable, his enunciation clear, no confusion or forgetfulness; it was just that he'd kept proposing and laying his kingdom at her feet.

His imaginary kingdom . . . or so she supposed. Granted, the man had certainly thrown money around with abandon. And he was well dressed. But when a stranger started offering a woman Learjets and Hope diamonds, it was, thought Raven, time to be wary. Amused, but wary.

Raven knew very well she was no victim of the Cinderella complex. She neither expected nor desired some handsome prince to sweep her off her feet and into a life of leisure. In the first place, twenty-eight years of life had convinced her that princes, handsome or otherwise, were in short supply in the circles in which she often found herself. In the second place, a life of leisure would drive her mad within a week.

Reluctantly, then, she remembered Josh Long clad only in a slipping towel. Tall and lean, his broad-shouldered and muscled frame spoke convincingly of a busy, physically active life. And his strikingly handsome face, with its sensual mouth and warm, vivid blue eyes had been designed for women to stare at.

There was about him an aura of confidence and power that had not been lessened in the least by inebriated proposals, comical one-sided discussions with wooden Indians, and a fiercely competitive arm-wrestling match. Drunk or sober, he moved like a cat . . . or a king—gracefully, proudly, powerfully, deceptively unhurried. He was the kind of man whom others would instinctively make way for.

Raven shook her head bemusedly. Impossible to ignore the man. If he wasn't a prince, he was certainly every woman's image of tall, dark, and handsome. And she had to admit to being flattered that even in his concussed and/or demented state he'd focused the power of those warm blue eyes on her.

The bacon was burning. Swearing, Raven turned the strips.

However, she simply hadn't the time or energy

to cope with a lunatic suitor with delusions of grandeur, no matter how handsome and charming he was.

His straightforward charm, though, was what she would most regret losing. Granted, she favored blue eyes and dark men, and she was woman enough to fully appreciate handsome men, but it was his charm she found so intriguing. The men who peopled her own world tended to have little charm, and the games they played were dangerous ones.

Games. Deadly serious games.

Raven sighed and put visions of intensely blue eyes out of her mind. There was no *time*, just no time for personal wishes.

Sighing, Raven arranged the bacon on paper towels to drain.

And, having decided to put unproductive thoughts out of her mind, she promptly began musing once again on his behavior of the night before.

She was a tall woman, yet he was taller and certainly much stronger; he hadn't used that strength in order to get what he clearly wanted—she'd seen desire in men's eyes before, and had recognized it in his intense gaze. He had proposed countless times in various ways, chased her playfully around a table or two, and told anyone who'd listen that she was going to marry him. By turns grave and comical, he had gotten everyone in the tavern to cheer him on.

But at no time was his pursuit in any way clumsy or crude. If he swore, it was mildly and with no heat. Far from making any physical pass, he had touched only her hand—and that with a curious kind of courtly deference and restraint that had been strangely moving and had made her oddly aware of restraint. Not a single vulgar word or crass joke had escaped his lips. And in spite of her amused rejection of his proposals, he had remained amiably determined.

All that—and he'd been quite wonderfully drunk.

"Marry me."

He didn't seem to be much different sober. Raven turned and surveyed his tall, dark, and handsome self as he stood in the kitchen doorway. Jeans, she decided, suited him admirably. In fact, if they'd suited him any *more* admirably, he'd have gotten mobbed in the streets by rabid women.

Raven ignored her weak knees just as she'd ignored them when he had appeared in a towel. "Coffee's over there," she said, gesturing. "Help yourself. Breakfast is ready."

Josh headed for the coffee, apparently undisturbed by this continual rejection. "Do you need coffee to start the day?" he asked with interest. "I do."

Setting two filled plates on the neat oak table, Raven murmured, "Then maybe you'll be rational in a little while." She didn't sound very hopeful.

"I'm rational now," he said, holding her chair.

Disconcerted, Raven sat with more haste than grace. She'd met men with manners, yes, but at *breakfast*?

He set coffee before them both, then took his own chair. "So tell me why we're in an apartment that isn't yours," he said chattily.

Raven gazed into his warm blue eyes for a moment, then began eating. "*We* are here," she said, "because I'm staying here while my friends are back east. You're here because the only identification you were carrying last night didn't name a Los Angeles address. You don't even carry a driver's license with you—just business cards with your name and a phone number."

Josh didn't tell her that he rarely needed any other identification. "I'm visiting," he explained, digging in to his own meal with every sign of enjoyment.

"From where?" she asked, wondering at her own curiosity. Was it because she wanted to get rid of him? Or because she wanted to understand this strangely intense, completely charming man?

"I spend most of my time in New York. How about you? A native of Los Angeles?"

"No," she said. "Where are you staying?"

"A hotel. Where *are* you from, then?"

"Back east. Which hotel?"

"Downtown. Where back east?"

Parry and thrust.

Raven bit back a giggle. Placidly, she said, "I was born in a Gypsy caravan in Romania, except that *really* I was the child of a baron, stolen by the Gypsies. He'd thrown them off his land, you see, so they decided to get revenge by stealing me. But they already had too many mouths to feed, so they sold me to an Irishman who needed a dancer in his tavern. Then one day while I was dancing on the bar, a Greek shipping tycoon wandered in and offered me a job being the target for a knife thrower in his circus. The Irishman wouldn't sell me, so the Greek bought the tavern with all contents included—meaning me—and spirited me away to London, then to the States. For a year I dodged knives, until the knife thrower pierced my left ear by mistake and I ran away. I ended up on a Mississippi riverboat, where a dissolute gambler taught me how to cheat at cards and look good in feathers. But it turned out that I was allergic to feathers and my nose quivered revealingly whenever I stacked a deck, so I left there and became a guide taking tourists to the floor of the Grand Canyon on muleback. After three trips I became a victim of vertigo, so that ended that job. I then hopped a freight train, headed west, and fell in love with Los Angeles at first sight. There didn't seem to be much demand for tavern dancers, targets for knife throwers, untalented gamblers allergic to feathers, or mule riders, so I ended up being a computer programmer at IBM."

Josh burst out laughing.

Raven, who had talked very quickly as she'd spun the tale out of thin air and a vivid imagination, took a deep breath, a sip of coffee, then asked gently, "And how was *your* life?"

"Boring, compared to yours," he told her.

"You mean you're not going to give me any of the details?" She was incredulous. "After I bared my soul and past to your cruel laughter?"

"I'm trying to entice you with my mystery," he explained gravely.

"It isn't working."

"Well, dammit, you seem to be above bribery; you were hardly impressed by the offer of my kingdom. An aura of mystery isn't getting me anywhere. My bare and manly chest obviously didn't affect you; you removed half my clothes last night and apparently felt not one pang of lust, and when I paraded before you clothed only in a towel, you never so much as blinked."

Raven choked on a laugh.

"I see I haven't been going about this the right way." Purposefully, Josh rose from his chair, came around the table, and took her arms to pull her up from her chair. "Clearly, what is needed here," he said sternly, "is a little old-fashioned persuasion." And he bent his dark head to hers.

Two

Caught off guard, Raven didn't have a chance to struggle. And, bewildering though the thought was, she wasn't at all certain that she would have struggled, given the chance. His lean, handsome face filled her vision, his arms closed around her, and Raven found her body swaying toward this stranger as though drawn by an irresistible magnet.

Even remembering his exemplary behavior of the night before, she half-expected an onslaught, a passionate demand. But when his lips met hers, it was with a gentle, seeking, almost tentative touch, soft and warm. Her body, braced for abrupt shock, found instead an insidious sweet warmth, and she felt her bones melting. Seduced, her mouth opened to his and her arms lifted to encircle his lean waist.

His head lifted a moment later, and Raven gazed rather dreamily into blue eyes that were hot now instead of warm. "This," she said, "has got to stop." Something told her the statement should have emerged more forcefully, and she tried again. "I mean it. I don't kiss strangers. Especially first thing in the morning." Not much better, she decided critically.

Josh smiled very slowly and his head bent again. And this time the demand came, hot and urgent. His lips slanted hungrily across hers while his hard arms pulled her so close she could feel the strong male contours of his body imprinting themselves on her own quivering flesh. Her senses exploded in a violent burst of inner sparks, the stark possession of his tongue and the pressure of his body against hers igniting something red hot and powerful deep inside of her.

She made a soft sound in the back of her throat without meaning to, her hands clutching his back, moving unconsciously to press herself even closer.

For a moment it seemed as though he would accept her mindless invitation. His mouth grew even more fierce, his arms tightening around her— and then he suddenly lifted his head and stared down at her with feverish blue eyes. "That doesn't happen between strangers," he said roughly. "Marry me, Raven."

There was nothing playful or amiable about him now, nothing to be taken as an amusing jest; he was utterly and completely serious, and she knew it. Within two seconds she also knew she was in trouble. The distant cool part of her mind began working with its hard-won logic, presenting one problem after another to her with depressing clarity. And there was no time . . . no time at all. She carefully dropped her arms and stepped back away from him, gathering the threads of control tight until her breathing steadied and she could trust her voice.

"Sometimes it does," she said, and made it sound like a statement of experience. "They call it chemistry. Finish your breakfast, Josh."

He sat down as she did, but didn't seem perturbed. "I'll convince you," he said easily. "I'm a patient man, and I've got all the time in the world." He wondered, on some dim and distant plane of his mind, how on earth he could sound so calm. His heart was pounding, and every thudding beat of it urged him to take her in his arms again and finish what he'd started.

Raven wanted to tell him that he might have time, but she didn't. However, experience had taught her only too well the dangers of confiding in anyone. She made her protest a dry and commonplace one. "I'm afraid I have little spare time," she told him. "I have to earn my living, which demands the bulk of the day."

"What do you do?" he asked casually.

"I'm a secretary." She had long ago stopped crossing her fingers while saying that. It no longer bothered her to lie. "A temporary secretary; I tend to have odd hours, and I take jobs within a three-hundred-mile radius of Los Angeles. What do you do?"

He grinned suddenly, his expression peculiarly amused. "Told you. I run a kingdom."

"Oh, right." She shook her head with the air of someone who'd forgotten some tiny detail. "You did tell me that. Is it an international kingdom, or domestic?"

"Domestic mostly," he explained in a conversational tone. "But I do own most of an airline, and it's international."

"Uh-huh."

"You don't believe me."

She smiled gently. "How often does a woman meet a prince?"

He chuckled. "Well, it doesn't matter. You aren't the kind of woman to be impressed by money or power."

Finishing her breakfast more by rote than any sense of hunger, Raven rose and carried her plate to the sink. Along with all the other violent emotions tangling inside her, she felt vaguely uneasy. Josh Long didn't strike her as a braggart, and his talk of wealth was just a bit too matter-of-fact to be a delusion. Still, she told herself, it hardly made any difference. He'd be out of her life very soon now.

That was a depressing thought, she decided.

"You haven't told me your last name," he observed, carrying his plate to the sink.

Her hesitation was fleeting. "Anderson. Look, I have a lunch appointment for this afternoon. I can drive you to your hotel."

"Thank you," he said gravely.

All Raven's instincts warned her that there was absolutely nothing meek about this man, warned that he had no intention of vanishing from her life. She ignored the warning, and ignored the scornful voice that told her *why* she was ignoring it. "Keep the clothes," she offered lightly. "Jud won't miss them."

"Jud?"

"My friend's husband."

"Ah." He nodded, then stepped over to the phone on the kitchen wall, lifted the receiver, and briefly studied the plastic-covered strip bearing the number. Then he replaced the receiver and smiled at her. "Got it. I assume you want to leave now? I'll get my things." And he strode from the kitchen.

Frowning a bit, Raven stowed the plates in the dishwasher. She didn't doubt he'd memorized the phone number; he would probably make a mental note of the address when they left. "Damn," she murmured.

Oddly enough, the curse didn't sound as fierce as she wanted it to. Not nearly as fierce . . .

Almost half an hour later, she pulled her battered Pinto to a halt before the imposing glass-and-steel hotel he had named. The doorman, his well-trained face impassive, came forward, only to be waved away by Josh. Turning in the bucket seat, he gazed intently at her.

"Go out with me tonight?"

She kept the smile on her face. "Sorry, I'm booked."

"Then I'll call you." He leaned toward her suddenly, kissing her gently but with more than a hint of the raw fire he had earlier unleashed. "Tonight."

Raven said nothing. She watched him gracefully unfold his length from the cramped little car and shut the door, then waved vaguely and drove away. Several blocks down the street and out of sight, she pulled her car over to the curb and sat for a moment, contemplating her shaking hands. "What lousy timing," she murmured. "Damn."

She thought of the night before, of laughter

and an easy companionship she'd never known before. She thought of warm blue eyes and a passion that still tingled within her. She thought of proposals, drunken and sober. Then she thought of a phone ringing in an empty apartment.

Swearing in a soft, toneless voice, she pulled back out into traffic and went on her way.

"I never made it to the party," Raven said. She was sitting at a picnic table, the paper clutter of lunch between her and the man opposite. Absently, she poked a finger at the horn-rimmed glasses slipping down her nose.

"Why not?" His voice was low and deep and his face boasted the open, ingenuous expression of a man with no secrets and few wits. It was a deceptive expression, to say the least.

Raven studied him for a moment in silence, although she knew his face almost as well as her own. "Well, ridiculous as it sounds, Kelsey, I knocked a man down in the hall at the hotel."

Kelsey ran blunt fingers through rusty hair. "You would. Did you kill him?"

"Funny." She decided not to explain the remainder of the night. "Anyway, I missed the party."

"There'll be questions."

"Yes. I know what I'll say, don't worry."

He nodded, then pushed a flat envelope across the table toward her. While she casually studied the contents, he studied her. Not a strand of her long black hair showed beneath the drab brown wig she wore, and her loose blouse and shabby jeans effectively shrouded a figure that normally caught every eye in passing. The heavy-rimmed glasses changed her features remarkably, leaving her with a curiously harried, fretful appearance, which was enhanced by her frequent, seemingly nervous gesture of pushing the rim up her nose.

Her own mother would have passed her without a glance.

"Travers having you followed?" he asked.

Raven shook her head, still gazing down at photographs. "No, not now. He was at first, so I stayed close to the penthouse and perfected my ice-maiden act. He relaxed a bit after a few days." She looked up at Kelsey, expressionless. "The background checked out, I imagine. I'm still being careful, though. No need to take chances now."

Kelsey snorted softly. "I certainly hope the background checked out. God knows it took us enough time. When will you make your move?"

She returned the photographs to their envelope and pushed it back across the table, stirring restlessly. "I don't know. He's leaving L.A. tonight, and last time he had men watching my place while he was out of town. I bet he will again. So I'll behave myself while he's gone, then see how things look when he gets back."

"Watch your step," Kelsey warned needlessly. "He's a barracuda with a full set of teeth."

She smiled a little. "I know. I'll be careful."

"You've got the pictures?" he asked.

"Of course." Raven tapped her forehead lightly with a finger. "Right here. I'll know when the time comes."

It was Kelsey's turn to move restlessly. Almost to himself, he said, "If he sticks with his normal mode of operation, the merchandise will leave the country within the next month or so. You don't have much time, Raven."

She knew.

Late that afternoon, Raven drove her battered Pinto into a private garage and parked it beside a gleaming silver Mercedes. The garage was deserted, and she moved swiftly and expertly within the car before getting out and stowing a small case where the spare tire should have been at the rear of the Pinto. She stood there for a minute, smoothing her long black hair and adjusting the silk dress. Then she put on a pair of mirrored sunglasses, slung an expensive leather handbag into the Mercedes, and got in herself.

She drove uptown to a towering apartment building and pulled up in front, smiling politely at the doorman, who rushed to open her door. "Thank you, Evan," she said, her tone low and cultured.

"My pleasure, Miss Anderson." The doorman escorted her up the tiled steps while a valet appeared from thin air and hurried to tenderly drive the Mercedes to its secluded parking place. A uniformed guard at the front desk rose respectfully to his feet as Raven entered, murmuring a greeting as he handed her a sheaf of messages.

"Mr. Travers is waiting for you, Miss Anderson."

The sunglasses hid Raven's expressive eyes that might have revealed how entirely unwelcome this information was. "Oh? Thank you," she commented. Gracefully, she moved to the elevator, where another uniformed man punched the buttons so that she wouldn't strain herself.

The door opened onto the top floor, and Raven

stepped out of the elevator with the gliding, feline movements she'd perfected. The grace was wasted, however, since she was forced almost immediately to jump to one side to avoid being run over by an untidy stack of papers and files with legs.

"Oh!" A harried, timid voice came from behind the obstruction, and a pale, thin face peered around at Raven. "Miss—Miss Anderson! I'm so sorry—"

"No harm done," she murmured, tempted, as always, to abandon her role, but resisting because experience had taught her caution. It certainly was difficult, though, to maintain her cool detachment in the presence of Leon Travers's assistant-or-whatever; she'd never been clear on the relationship.

Theodore Thorpe Thayer III was the optimistically grand name bestowed, possibly by a lisping mother, some thirty-odd years ago on the child who could never hope to equal it. Theodore—*never* Ted, Raven had decided—was about five foot four and might have weighed a hundred pounds on one of his hearty-eating days. He was pale, and his thin face invariably wore the expression of a hunted rabbit. And behind the cruelly distorting lenses of his glasses, spaniel-brown eyes pleaded with the whole world.

How on earth the amazingly inept man had secured a job with Leon Travers had been a total mystery to Raven until Leon had explained in a long-suffering tone that Theodore was related to him and, as he pointed out, who else would hire him?

Bringing her mind back to specifics, Raven asked coolly, "What are you doing here, Theodore?" The question was mild enough, but Theodore looked crushed.

"I'm—I'm sorry, Miss Anderson, but I thought Leon—I mean, Mr. Travers wanted to work here. I could have *sworn* he told me, but I was wrong." The spaniel eyes blinked rapidly behind thick lenses.

Raven glanced back over her shoulder, where the elevator operator, expressionless, was still waiting. She looked at Theodore. "Did you really think you could accomplish all that anyway?" she asked dryly, gesturing to the stack of work he clutched to his chest.

Theodore promptly lost himself in a morass of unfinished sentences and stuttered explanations, none of which made the least bit of sense.

Raven waved it away. "Never mind. The elevator's waiting, Theodore."

He nodded miserably and scurried into it.

When she stepped into her penthouse apartment a few moments later, Raven smiled far more welcomingly than she had at the doorman, but there was an almost imperceptible chill in the curve of her lips, stamped there, it seemed, as a glacier permanently stamped its mark on the soft earth beneath it.

"Hello, Leon."

"I used my key," he said.

The phone rang endlessly in the empty apartment.

Josh counted the rings, hanging up when he reached twenty. She wasn't there. He had called from ten P.M. last night until two this morning, then had given up. Waking after a restless night, he had begun calling at eight this morning; it was Saturday, she shouldn't be working.

Three hours ago he had driven his rented car to the apartment she was supposed to be living in. The manager had been shocked by the very idea; the tenants were back east, she'd said, but there was no sublet, no helpful friend watching the place for them. Raven Anderson? She'd never heard of her.

Josh lit a cigarette, not, by far, the first of the day, and stared broodingly at the phone. Well, hell, he hadn't imagined it. He remembered ripe curves and warm lips far too clearly for it to have been a dream or a drunken delusion—and he wasn't given to imagining things.

Nor had his body forgotten. He still felt that new, strangely vivid sensitivity, the feeling that everything inside him was focused intensely on her. Restlessness and frustration were making him jittery, uncomfortable—and he had never been a man to let his emotions manifest themselves physically. But these emotions were growing more powerful by the moment, even without the sight or touch of her to feed the hunger; his mind was filled with vivid images that had haunted him since he had first seen her.

Images of beautiful violet eyes and gleaming black hair, of tender lips curved in amusement and faintly swollen from his passion. Images of full breasts lovingly restrained by a blue dress and lending a seductive shape to a bulky sweater. Images of curved hips and long legs . . .

He lifted his gaze to look around the penthouse suite, barely taking notice; he had been in too many far too similar suites for the architecture or decor to make any impression on him.

The desk where he sat was near wide, floor-to-ceiling windows running the length of one wall. The floor was sunken, an off-white pit grouping allowing seating space for a small convention and a fireplace offering more than electric or gas heat. A far-from-compact bar stood in one corner, and two closed doors hinted that there were at least that many bedrooms and quite likely more.

In short, it was a very large suite.

From one of the bedrooms stepped a man whom most people would cross the street to avoid. It wasn't only that he was several inches over six feet and tended to fill doorways; it wasn't even that a wicked scar twisted down his lean cheek. What it was about the man that frightened even the stouthearted was a palpable aura of leashed power and an atmosphere of cold menace.

He moved like a big cat as he came into the room, as if he walked on dried leaves and wished to be silent. And he would have been silent even with dried leaves underfoot. The immaculate business suit he wore did absolutely nothing to conceal the danger of him, nor did the calm, almost bland expression on his rugged face or the serene gray eyes.

Josh focused on the man. "Zach," he said slowly, "I've got a job for you."

His security chief, sometimes bodyguard, and friend of fifteen years eased his considerable bulk into a chair by the desk. "We aren't going on?" he asked equably.

"No. I've canceled the remainder of the trip."

"Then put me to work." The big man's voice was curiously soft.

Having made up his mind, Josh began speaking rapidly, concisely. "I want you to do a background check on a woman named Raven Anderson. Waist-length black hair, violet eyes, tall, striking. Late twenties, I'd say. Says she's from back east somewhere." He described her car and rattled off the license plate, then gave the address of the apartment and phone number. "The manager claims the apartment is empty, not sublet, but Raven knew where everything was in the kitchen."

Zach had not made notes, but he wouldn't forget; he possessed a phenomenal memory. He didn't ask Josh why he wanted the background, nor did he think for a moment that it was because of personal interest. His friend and employer's aversion to brunettes was well known, and had stopped being a joke years ago.

"Pull some of the team in if you need to," Josh was saying as he restlessly lit another cigarette. "I don't care what it costs. Just find out."

"Right." Zach rose soundlessly from his chair and left the room, prepared to do anything on the right side of legal to get the information. Josh Long was perhaps the only truly honest man Zach had ever known. Left to himself, Zach would probably have crossed into the gray area that was the despair of judges and courtrooms, but he knew his employer too well.

And because of Josh's somewhat unusual background, it wasn't necessary. In every major law enforcement agency the country could boast, Josh Long merely had to ask to be granted instant and complete cooperation.

Los Angeles was no exception.

Still, it took hours. Zach decided not to call in the team of investigators and security men he had built over the years to handle some of the more complex aspects of Josh Long's empire. Instead, he requested of hotel management—and was instantly granted—a small office off the lobby complete with computer and phone linkup, and went to work.

Computers were one of Zach's many areas of expertise, and he carried in his mind access codes the federal government tended to be possessive about. He hardly expected to find anything earth-shattering . . . but what he found was quite definitely interesting.

Just before midnight, Zach returned to the sunken den of the suite, carrying a computer printout of some length. He found Josh seated at his desk, having obviously just hung up the phone, a frown on his face.

"Well?" Josh never snapped, but that came close to it.

Zach came forward to place the printout before his boss. He was understandably pleased with himself, since he had spent hours not only gathering information from several data centers, but also confirming every fact. "I wouldn't recommend reading this before bedtime," he said in his soft, pleasant voice. "Give you nightmares."

Josh sent him a sharp look, then bent his dark head to study the printout.

Zachary Steele, in the opinion of all who knew him, was afraid of nothing that walked on earth.

But as he watched Josh reading, he began to feel very edgy. He knew his employer and friend well, but he had never seen anything like the utter stillness slowly gripping that lean face. He quite unconsciously braced himself, powerful muscles growing taut, and had sudden visions of heads lopped off and flying across hotel rooms. One head, at least. His own. He was abruptly glad he had made up his will years before.

Josh looked up. "What the hell is this?" he asked softly.

It took all the will Zach could command not to blink at the fixed, intense rage in those normally cool and calm blue eyes. But he had to clear his throat before he could speak. "Background on Raven Anderson. I verified every fact."

"Then you've got the wrong woman." Josh's voice was flat and hard.

Zach hesitated, then reached into the inner pocket of his jacket and unfolded a sheet of stiff paper. "I called and requested a wire photo. Picked it up a little while ago." He placed the sheet on the desk faceup.

Josh could scarcely bear to look. Through his mind swam the madness of what he had read. A long list of aliases going back ten years. Indictments—but no convictions—for grand theft, forgery, fraud, solicitation for the purposes of prostitution . . . The FBI listed her as a possible subversive, linking her with a terrorist group but claiming no proof. And the CIA believed that now she was representing "international interests" in the area of white slavery.

Madness . . .

"Her present address," Zach said woodenly, feeling skewered by those eyes and wondering why Josh hadn't looked at the photo, "is a penthouse in a very exclusive highrise here in L.A. The lease is held by Leon Travers."

Slowly, every inch a stabbing agony, Josh looked down at the picture. It was grainy, but clear for all of that. A young woman with icy eyes holding a numbered card in front of her. And below the photo was printed height, weight, coloring, general description. The report of an identifying scar on her lower back, the wound gained during a knife fight.

It was Raven.

"Thank you, Zach." Josh's voice was toneless now. "Your usual . . . thorough job."

Zach hesitated for a moment, then turned and silently left the room, bothered by what he had left behind.

Josh drew out his lighter and held the printout to the flame. When the last charred ashes in the glass tray on his desk heaped to overflowing, he burned the picture. Not that it mattered, since the efficient Zach would have made duplicate copies of both. And he couldn't burn the words or the image in his mind of a striking face with merry eyes, an image not even the harsh photo could replace. He turned off his desk lamp and sat in the darkness, gazing sightlessly out over the glittering lights of the city far below.

.

"Man was here asking about you, Raven."

She unlocked the apartment door, but paused to smile at the manager. "When, Liz?"

"Saturday. Told him the apartment was empty

and I'd never heard of you." Her sharp brown eyes were steady on Raven's face. "Seemed a bit upset, but a very nice man." She described Josh Long briskly, adding in satisfaction, "A hunk."

Raven laughed. "You've been watching too much television! And stop guarding me like a cat with one kitten and trying to marry me off."

Liz sniffed. "High time you were married, at your age."

It was a frequent comment, and Raven only smiled, waved, and disappeared into her apartment. Then she poked her head out as Liz was turning to leave and whispered conspiratorially, "He *is* a hunk, though, isn't he?"

She thought about her own words later, disturbed by the flare of excitement she'd felt in knowing Josh had come searching for her. But that would never do. He'd ruin everything if he started asking questions about her. She felt a sudden chill, thinking of another handsome face, this one topped by silver hair and wearing a constant, beneficent smile.

Though dangerous, it was entirely necessary for her to return here from time to time, here, where there was no taint of Leon Travers's deceptively charming presence, and where she could relax her ever-present guard. He would be in meetings all day today, so she had a few hours to relax and unwind before she had to be back at the penthouse to meet him for dinner tonight.

The thought of hours without the strain of performance made her voice light and cheerful when she answered the pealing demand of the phone. "Hello?"

There was an instant of silence, and then a deep, oddly husky voice. "Raven? It's Josh."

She caught her breath and silently commanded her heart to quit pounding so erratically. "Oh—hello, Josh."

"You've been gone."

Raven licked her lips nervously, wondering what Kelsey would think of the betraying gesture. "Yes, a job out of town."

"I'd like to see you."

She watched her fingers twisting the phone cord. "I have plans for tonight."

"How about now? I'll get a picnic lunch and we can go somewhere."

"All—all right." Was that shy voice really hers? A part of her mind was working swiftly. Where could they avoid being seen? "I know a place."

"Pick you up in an hour." He hung up.

Raven cradled the receiver slowly. So. She was, she knew, being incredibly stupid, rash, and insanely reckless. She was putting lives in danger, including her own.

And Josh's.

She looked around the bright, cheerful apartment, and became conscious, not for the first time, of walking a tightrope between two worlds. Her neighbors in this area and the other few friends she had made considered her a laughing and carefree young woman with a penchant for taking in strays—animal and human. Someone who was quick to offer a loan and who, when not out of town on one of her frequent "business trips" was always willing to watch neighborhood kids for an hour or take shut-ins out for groceries or a visit to a park or theater.

And at that other apartment building across town she was known as a wealthy, somewhat mysterious woman with a chill manner. A woman, it was also known, whom the police would have given much to question at length and without the limitations of law. A woman representing those who trafficked in human lives and who was herself invisibly but unalterably tarred with their evil brush.

A woman who might or might not be Leon Travers's mistress.

Abruptly, Raven hurried through the apartment toward the shower. She felt dirty.

When Zach came into the den, he walked even more lightly than usual. For the past several days he had walked lightly even for him. It was not that Josh had been throwing objects or roaring his displeasure; Zach could have accepted that, though it would have surprised him, since open temper was not a part of his friend's personality.

No, what had been happening these last days was much quieter and far more devastating than temper. Josh was not given to excess, but Zach had watched him drinking steadily; what was so unnerving about it was that he never got drunk. He had eaten what was put before him without seeming to notice his actions, yet had lost several pounds and it all showed in his face. He was, Zach thought, finely honed, sharpened, stretched almost to the breaking point.

Zach had seen men under stress of battle who looked like that, and he knew the dangers of it. But he was powerless. Josh had faced too many unpleasant truths in his life to allow someone else to cushion a blow for him—even if that were possible.

But now, moving lightly into the den, Zach was relieved to find something had changed. Josh was freshly showered and shaved, and he was talking on the phone, asking the hotel to pack a picnic lunch for two. Zach waited, and since he was not a man who had to be brained with a two-by-four to see something that would have been obvious to a blind man, he was not surprised by his friend's flat statement to him.

"I don't believe it." Josh stood by his desk, one hand still resting on the phone, and his eyes were clear for the first time in days. "I can't be that wrong about someone. Zach, pull in the team. Pull every string you can find, call in every favor. I want every fact in that damned dossier verified by a dozen sources, and then I want *them* verified. Don't take anyone's word for anything. Get our investigators checking her background in person." He drew a deep breath. "This is a very personal matter to me—and I don't care who knows it."

Zach opened his mouth to speak, but Josh was gone. The big security man stood frowning for a moment. He had never known Josh to miss a point, but Zach thought he might have missed this one because he was too close to the problem.

Still, Zach got on the phone and began calling out the troops. But he had reservations. If Raven Anderson's background somehow had been fabricated, the question uppermost in Zach's mind was *why*.

Why would she need a background like that?

• • •

During the first hour he was with Raven again, Josh was conscious of a feeling of unreality. She was the woman he'd met in the hallway of a hotel, lovely and cheerful, with a wry sense of humor and laughing eyes. With little help from him, she kept the conversation going, never referring to her absence or betraying, by so much as a flicker of her eye, the double life she might well be leading.

And his body, at least, didn't give a damn whether or not she *was* leading a double life. The increasingly familiar aching throb of desire intensified the moment she opened the apartment door, and grew steadily moment by moment. Tension wound tightly within him and his mouth was dry.

The stress of the last days had left his emotions ragged and painful, and the growing desire found a firm hold. He was half out of his mind with wanting her, and he was dimly aware he needed some kind of reassurance that she was what he believed her to be.

Following her directions, he drove to a serene little park, where they spread a blanket beneath an oak tree and enjoyed the lunch his hotel's chef had provided.

Josh couldn't take his eyes off her, and struggled to maintain the certainty he'd felt earlier. She was dressed in jeans and a sleeveless sweater, her glorious hair unbound and shining; her striking face was free of makeup and needed none.

Solicitation for the purposes of prostitution . . .

"Your apartment manager said she didn't know you," he said abruptly, looking down at the blade of grass he was twisting between his fingers.

Raven smiled easily. "I'm sorry. I should have

warned you. Liz is very protective. A couple of weeks ago, some nut followed me home a few times, then tried to find out from Liz which apartment I lived in. She called the police, and they advised her to deny that any single woman lived in the building."

"I see." It was, he thought, plausible.

"It backfired once," Raven added. "There's another single woman who lives upstairs, and when a rejected boyfriend came calling, Liz told him the place had been sublet. What she didn't know was that, to put it mildly, the guy was on the shady side. He broke in one night and grabbed everything he could carry—and he honestly didn't know it was his former girlfriend he was ripping off."

She studied Josh, wondering what was different about him. He looked leaner, she thought, and somewhat preoccupied; there was an almost imperceptible distance in his manner, a guarded distance. With an unexpected twinge of pain, she realized that his intent though cheerful pursuit of her apparently had burned itself out within these last days.

Telling herself that was for the best did absolutely nothing to ease her depression.

"Are you subletting?" he asked in an idle tone. "Or just staying in the apartment while your friends are gone?"

"Just staying there." She forced a smile. "How about you? About ready to leave L.A. and go take care of the kingdom?"

Josh's face was oddly still when he lifted his gaze to meet hers, and his smile seemed not to touch unreadable blue eyes. "No, I'm staying here for a while. I have to find out if my . . . my Waterloo will break me in the end."

Raven felt her heart lurch, but told herself that he couldn't possibly mean what she thought he did. "Cryptic comments over the potato salad," she said lightly, gesturing toward the repacked wicker basket on the corner of the blanket.

"Was I cryptic? Sorry." This time the smile did touch his eyes. "Just thinking of that old saying that every man meets his Waterloo sooner or later. I met mine the other night in the hallway of a hotel."

He *did* mean . . . Raven cleared her throat. "Josh—"

"You said you didn't have a lover."

She couldn't look away from those intent, searching eyes. "No. But I'm involved in business right now. I don't have time for a relationship."

"Make time."

It was hardly an imperious demand, she reflected. It was something else. Something urgent and with a curious undertone of entreaty. Deep within her, she felt guarded walls begin to waver, and hastily shored them up again. It was *dangerous*—too dangerous—to get involved with him. There were too many problems.

"You're about to say no." Josh moved suddenly, stretching out beside her where she lay on her side, guiding her gently until she lay on her back. "Don't say no."

He kissed her before she could speak, trying not to show her the desperation he felt, trying not to reveal the tangled threads of doubt and certainty, love and fear, belief and disbelief. And when her mouth warmed beneath his, responding instantly to him, he tried to forget everything but her . . . the touch of her . . . the taste of her. . . .

"Josh." It wasn't protest or invitation; it was simply the heart's driven instinct to say aloud a name that meant too much to say silently. She could feel muscles rippling beneath her fingers as he moved, the heat of him burning her even through the fine linen of his shirt. Burning. She could feel his fire, and every instinct warned that he was almost out of control. His lips seared a path down her throat until her sweater halted his progress, and she felt one of his hands slipping beneath the sweater at her waist.

Raven wanted to abandon herself, but then she caught a flicker of movement from the corner of her eye; there was someone in the trees only a few yards away. Even as she realized, her hand caught Josh's wrist and she felt like screaming in frustration. Kelsey. Damn him.

Josh had obeyed her hand, his own lying still on the warm flesh of her midriff. He kissed her, a hard and possessive kiss, then lifted his head to show her darkened, flaming eyes. "Not here, I agree," he murmured.

Raven knew why Kelsey had caught her attention; she didn't have to look at her watch. Gazing up at Josh and feeling torn almost in two, she said huskily, "I told you. I have an appointment tonight."

His slight smile vanished. "You won't break it." Not a question.

"I can't. I'm sorry, Josh. It's—it's business."

For the first time in his life Josh wanted to lose

control. He wanted to take her right here, now, lose himself in her until he went out of his mind with pleasure. He didn't want to think. He wanted her willing and wild beneath him, her body sheathing his in the heat of a primitive joining that would sear away all thought, all doubt.

But he fought silently and fiercely for control, knowing that to follow those instincts would be to betray her. And if he possessed her with such motives driving him, it could well destroy him.

When she began moving away, he didn't stop her. Instead, he rose also and helped her to gather up the blanket. Abruptly, compelled by his doubts and fears, he asked, "Do you know Leon Travers?"

Raven was bending to get the basket and answered idly, "I suppose everyone knows of him, but we've never met." She didn't see Josh wince as though she'd struck him.

Three

Raven didn't have time to contact Kelsey and find out why he'd been following her. Shortly after a very distant Josh had dropped her off at the apartment without saying good-bye, she drove her Pinto to the garage, exchanged it for the Mercedes, and transformed herself quickly and expertly for the role she had to play.

She was still quivering inside with the desire Josh evoked, and her heart pounded slowly and heavily with the realization that she could no longer even temporarily set aside thoughts about Josh Long. He was in her blood, in her mind and heart. She couldn't seem to think straight, and only the certain knowledge of how dangerous that was enabled her to head for the penthouse with some semblance of her normal control.

If only Josh would be patient for just a little while, she thought. A few weeks at most. Then they could be together without all this . . . trouble. Holding the steering wheel tightly, she wondered if she could find a way to get him out of town until this was finished. Maybe when she got a chance to contact Kelsey, they could find a way.

She thought of Josh's likely reaction to what she was doing, and shivered slightly. He wouldn't like it. No man would like it. So many lies she'd have to tell him, had already told him. And lies were hardly a foundation for a relationship, although the truth was even more dangerous. Instinct told her he was not a man who would care to be deceived; he could well learn to hate her once the truth was out.

Raven gripped the wheel even tighter and pulled into the drive of the towering apartment building. She couldn't think of that, couldn't let herself think of that. Drawing threads of control taut within her, she concentrated on the role.

Control, Zach decided silently. That was why they were sitting in a car an hour past midnight watching the front entrance of the apartment building across the street. They were here because Josh Long had what amounted to an obsession about keeping control of his life, and the woman presently in the penthouse of this building was shaking that control.

Zach glanced at the man in the passenger seat and silently amended the thought. *Destroying* that control. This strained, intense man was not the one who had come to Los Angeles. Zach tried, again, to dissuade his friend from what he planned to do. "There'll be a guard inside—"

"You studied the plans, didn't you? There has to be a quiet way past him."

Reluctantly, Zach said, "There's a service entrance, likely quiet this time of night." He paused, then added hopefully, "I'll have to bypass the alarm system to get you in."

"Then that's the way."

If Zach had been given to double-takes, he would have done one then; in fifteen years, he'd never known Josh to permit any of his people to break the law. The very thought had been anathema to him. "Illegal entry," Zach reminded him, but no longer hopefully; Josh was clearly willing to do whatever it took to get up to that penthouse secretly.

Josh didn't respond.

"If anyone sees you going into Leon Travers's building," Zach commented, "it'll really hurt your reputation as an honest businessman. Why don't you just call the lady and meet her somewhere?"

"I want to see her *there*," he said in a low voice, his gaze riveted to the entrance to the building. She told me she'd never met him; I want to face her with that where she can't deny it." He wasn't entirely sure why he was so adamant about reaching the penthouse unseen; perhaps it was simply because Travers was a dangerous man and Josh wanted to take no chances. There was, at least, that much of his control left.

"Going to tell her about the dossier?"

"No." Josh lit a cigarette. "I want her to tell me."

"Think that's likely?"

Josh swore, every word harshly expelled with smoke. "How the hell do I know? She seems to be living a damned double life, and there *must* be a reason for it."

Zach sent him a guarded look, then said carefully, "If the dossier was legit, maybe she just needs a clean place to wash off the dirt." He thought he'd gone too far for a moment; even in the darkness he caught the stabbing glance from the other side of the car.

"The report's wrong," Josh said gratingly. "*Wrong*. There's an explanation for it. There has to be."

His friend tried another tack. "And we'll find it, if it's there. Why don't you go on and finish the trip while we look into it? By the time you head back this way, we'll know. There's no hurry, is there?"

Josh stared briefly up at the lighted windows of the penthouse. "Travers is up there," he said savagely. "With her. If he's had his filthy hands on her—I have to know, Zach. About that, at least, I have to know."

"And the rest?" Zach deliberately made his tone of voice harsh. "D'you think you can live with that, if it's true? D'you think you could even touch her knowing she was a liar, a thief . . . a whore?" A choked sound came from the passenger seat, but Zach pushed on relentlessly. "You know what I found out today. You know that so far everything checks out. What if it *all* checks out?"

"It won't!" Josh drew a deep breath. "You haven't met her; I have. That file is about another woman, it has to be. Or it's a pack of lies."

"I guess we'll find out." Zach was staring toward the building's entrance. "There's Travers." They both watched the silver-haired man step into a gleaming limousine that drove away without lingering. "I guess you'll find out at least part of it tonight."

• • •

When Leon had gone, Raven took a quick shower and got ready for bed. She habitually wore a silk and lace teddy as sleepwear, and dressed now in a violet creation that left little to the imagination. Feeling a bit chilled in the air-conditioned penthouse, she also donned a white silk robe.

She went into the kitchen and made a pot of cocoa, then carried her cup into the den and gazed around restlessly. She didn't want to sleep, didn't want to dream. She debated between television and a book, deciding finally to read and listen to music. But instead of using the built-in stereo system the penthouse boasted, she got a portable tape player from her bedroom and set it carefully on a low table beside a large arrangement of silk flowers.

Though it hardly looked it, the small tape player had one special quality that Raven depended on whenever she felt it necessary to confuse listening ears: it was designed to damp out reception by electronic bugs like the one planted among the silk flowers.

Raven had made a habit of playing the tape recorder whenever she felt like listening to music. Habitual behavior tended to allay suspicion; by checking with his security people, Leon would know that she was alone, and had no reason to guard against being bugged. And she also needed at least occasional moments free of the sensation of someone listening to every sound she made.

Leon had examined the player—apparently casually but with real thoroughness—after she used it the first night. After that he had ignored it. Undoubtedly his electronics experts had assured him that the tape player was harmless, that it was beyond the present state of the art to build a machine that could overcome electronic listening devices. The expert who had built this one had assured her that his breakthrough invention was top secret.

When the doorbell rang, Raven froze. The guard downstairs had not announced a visitor. Kelsey? She went quickly to the door and peered through the peephole—and the frozen sensation she'd previously experienced was nothing compared to the cold she felt now. Icy hands moved to unlock and open the door, and she stared at Josh with a horror she could not conceal.

He brushed past her without a greeting, going into the den and turning in a slow circle to stare at the blatant wealth all around him. He looked at the stark white carpet that was ankle-deep, at the plush gray pit grouping, at glass-topped tables and oil paintings and fragile lamps and vases. Then he turned to stare at her as she came slowly nearer.

"So you don't know Leon Travers?" His voice was taut, the savagery held in check barely below the surface.

Raven drew the lapels of her robe tightly together and crossed her arms over her breasts, trying to think. "What are you doing here? How did you—"

"Answer me!"

The lash of that voice was enough, just barely enough, to jolt Raven's mind. She thought fleetingly of the man who after several drinks had laid his kingdom wistfully at her feet, comparing that gentle man—and gentleman—with this tautly controlled but obviously savage stranger. Not two different men, just two sides of one man.

She kept her voice steady with a tremendous effort. "I know him. I'm doing some work for him."

"What kind of *work*?"

Raven's chin came up swiftly, and only years of discipline enabled her to stop herself from reacting to the scorn and disgust in that final word. But it took everything she had . . . much more than she had ever needed before.

She spoke in a measured, impersonal tone. "Work. Since you seem to know this is his building—which, by the way, isn't commonly known—then you must be aware that Mr. Travers is very security-conscious. I wouldn't have a job very long if I told anyone who asked what my work entailed."

"This is his *penthouse*."

"No. He holds the lease, but if you're implying what I think you are, that he stays here, you're wrong. He sublets the place on a temporary basis to people who work for him. Like me."

"He left half an hour ago."

"We sometimes work here. Like tonight."

Josh wanted to believe her. God, how he wanted to. But he knew too many other apparent facts to let go of this so easily. "And the clothes?" he asked tightly, gesturing to her expensive sleepwear. "The car downstairs in the garage? Does he *sublet* those too?"

He watched her face drain of its remaining color, fighting the instincts urging him to go to her, gather her in his arms, tell her that he hadn't meant it, could never think she was—

"I'm not a whore." Her voice was very soft, toneless. The laughing violet eyes were dark and still, and her face was expressionless. "But you think what you like. You will anyway. Get out, Josh. Before I call the security people and have you thrown out." It was a bluff; the last thing in the world Raven would have done was call attention to his presence here.

Josh reached out to catch her shoulders, all but shaking her. "I don't want to believe it," he said thickly. "But you're *here* . . . dressed like this . . . and he just left. . . ." The smell of herbal soap rose from her skin, and Josh felt dizzy suddenly; his heart told him the woman he held couldn't possibly be what the dossier claimed, but the cool brain that had added immeasurably to an empire reminded him that some dirt couldn't be seen. "Raven . . ."

"Get out." Her voice was no longer steady.

"I can't." He thought distantly of Zach's warning and wondered what it would do to him if he found out she was what the report said she was. It didn't bear thinking of. "It's too late for me to get out."

She didn't understand what he meant; her mind had stopped working. And her protest was only a faint broken cry when he pulled her suddenly against him and captured her lips with an odd, despairing hunger.

Raven tried to fight, struggling in his arms with the devastating knowledge that he believed her to be something terrible. Others had believed the same thing; she had made certain of that. But for Josh to believe it hurt her dreadfully. She didn't want to respond to his passion . . . didn't want to feel this for a man who thought her a whore.

But the seductive magic of his touch sapped

even horror, and her body responded mindlessly. She felt him pulling aside the silk robe, and his lips pressed her shoulder, her throat. Her knees were weak, and she slid her arms around his neck, seeking the strength that he had and she had lost.

His mouth found hers again, his head slanting to deepen the contact, his tongue touching hers and demanding a response. He kissed her as though she were his for the taking, and he intended to take . . . and take. . . . Raven had never felt such utter certainty radiating from a man, such primitive determination, and she couldn't fight him or the shivers of pleasure and excitement that were shaking her body.

And Josh, holding the vital, responsive woman tightly against his own hardening, heating body, knew dimly that he was again on the edge of totally losing control. He was no longer conscious of even faint surprise that she held the power to do this to him, the power to ignite his body and shake his mind. He was aware only of building need, the surging fire of a ragged and overpowering desire.

And it wasn't just a woman he wanted. He wanted *her*, Raven. The muscles of his belly contracted and his legs were rigid with tension as he widened them and pulled her even closer, one hand sliding over her silk-clad back to her hips, pressing her yielding warmth into full and aching contact with his swelling body.

"I don't believe it," he muttered hoarsely against her skin. "I can't believe it. I couldn't feel this way if you weren't what I think you are."

"Josh . . ."

He was moving against her subtly, one hand pressing her hips to his strongly, the other tangled in her long hair, kissing her deeply again and again. "I want you until I can't think straight," he breathed. "Until I can't see anything but you, feel anything but you."

Every breath rasping harshly in his throat, Josh held her, kissed her, touched her compulsively. But even though she responded to every touch, he could feel, at first dimly, that she was holding back. And he remembered belatedly what he had accused her of, remembered that he had all but said aloud what no man should ever say to a woman. Not something she could forget, even in the mindless heat of passion . . .

His tongue caught the salt of tears on her cheeks, mute testimony that he was right, and it shook him badly. "Don't! I'm sorry I hurt you."

Hurt. It gave Raven the strength to pull away from him, the thought of who would be hurt if she allowed Josh to distract her from what she had to do. Crying . . . why was she crying? She hadn't realized. She turned away, rubbing her wet cheeks with the backs of her hands and retying her robe, then sank down on the couch with an unsteady sigh. "Get out," she whispered.

He sat down beside her, catching her hand when she would have moved away. "I can't, Raven. I can't leave while you think—I'm sorry about what I said. So sorry. Please believe that."

She shook her head a little, trying to think. "I believe you're sorry, but you can't take back the words. Or the doubt. It doesn't make for a good beginning, Josh. Just let it stop here, all right?"

"No." He lifted a hand to her face, making her

look at him. His breathing was only beginning to steady, and his voice was deep and husky. "I told you I was a patient man; somehow, I'll make it up to you for what I said tonight. I won't walk out of your life, Raven."

Raven looked at him and knew she was lost, knew she would do everything in her power to keep him safe—except let him walk away. She couldn't do that. Not even to save either of them. "Then there's something you have to understand. And something you have to promise me."

"Anything," he said instantly.

She glanced around at the opulent apartment. "This part of my life is separate. You can't be a part of it. When I'm in the other apartment, I can see you. But not here. Never again here."

He was frowning. "But you won't tell me why?"

"I can't. For—for security reasons. If you can't accept that, then it's no good." *Tell me you can't accept that! Walk away from me before I destroy us both!*

"Raven—"

"I mean it! I know it's a lot to ask, that—that everything looks and sounds bad, but you'll just have to decide if you trust me. And that's all." *A lot to ask!* Her mind sneered at her. With the evidence all around him, no man would trust her as she asked. No man could trust her.

Josh looked into those steady, beautiful, hurting violet eyes and knew right then, in that moment, that no matter how bad things appeared, he did, in fact, trust her. Doubts and uncertainties faded away. "All right." He smiled crookedly. "I think I forgot to mention it, but I love you."

She was shaken, and looked it. "Josh, don't say

that. Everything is so complicated right now. I can't even think."

"I have to say it." He leaned forward to kiss her gently. "But I won't say it again until you're ready to hear it." He released her, then reached into his pocket and withdrew a business card and a pen. He turned the card over and jotted a number quickly, then handed her the card. "This is my phone number at the hotel. Will you promise to call me as soon as you're back in the other apartment?"

She nodded, unable to do anything else.

He rose to his feet, then hesitated as he looked down at her. Dear Lord, he couldn't bear to leave her! "Will it be very long?"

Raven met his look as steadily as she could. "Days. I'm usually here for days at a time."

His jaw tightened, but he nodded. "I'll wait." He headed for the door, pausing when he reached it to turn and gaze at her. "No one will know I was here; I came up the back way, and that's how I'll leave." Then he was gone.

Raven stared at the door for long moments, still aware of the warmth of his touch, still seeing the sudden gentleness of his eyes. She was vaguely conscious of the music that had played steadily while he was with her, the machine automatically restarting itself after playing one side of the tape. And in the back of her mind, a small voice spoke up wryly. *No wonder Hagen said I'd be no good to him once I fell in love.*

She had taken that step; there was no going back. None of her painfully won defenses had been able to stand against him; she couldn't fight what

she felt. And Raven wondered what—and whom—
she might have sacrificed to love a man.

"No more cavorting in parks," Kelsey told her
cheerfully when they met quietly two days later.
"You seemed a bit distracted, so I thought you
might have needed reminding that we're on a
tight schedule."

"I'm glad you did." They were in a museum, and
Raven was gazing at the large abstract painting
on the wall near the bench on which they sat. The
huge room was deserted except for them.

Kelsey sent her a thoughtful look. "I couldn't
help but wonder who he was."

"Don't give me that. You ran his license plate."

He chuckled. "So I did. Car's a rental."

"Yes. So?"

"So," Kelsey said softly, "I got back a lot of
gibberish from the computer."

Raven turned her head slowly and stared at
him. "The rental company would have had an
agreement—"

"You'd think. But I couldn't trace that plate.
Oh, the company acknowledged the car was theirs,
but they said it was being serviced, not rented."

The hollow feeling inside Raven grew. "His name
is Joshua Long," she said quietly. "At least that's
what he told me, and I saw an ID." She remembered then, and added slowly, "Just a business
card with his name and a phone number. A New
York number, I think." He'd given her a card, but
Raven didn't have it with her and couldn't remember the phone number.

"Rings a bell." Kelsey frowned. "He's not from L.A.? Where's he staying?"

She told him. She was simultaneously close to laughter and tears now that it was her turn to suspect Josh of being something other than he seemed. She didn't like the uncertainty. She didn't like it at all.

"How'd you meet him?"

"He's the man I knocked down in the hotel."

Plainly worried, Kelsey ran fingers through his hair. "I'll check him out. Meantime, I hope you sent him on his way." When she remained silent, his voice sharpened. "Raven?"

"I'll see him only at home," she said softly, not about to tell Kelsey that Josh had found her in Leon Travers's penthouse.

Kelsey felt faint surprise, but only because it hadn't happened until now; he'd always known Raven would fall hard when she finally did fall. "I'll check him out—quickly," he said.

"I still don't understand what I'm doing here," Rafferty Lewis complained to Zach as they sat in the den of Josh's suite. "I'm an attorney, not a detective." His humorous brown eyes flicked a glance at the third man in the room, a rather strikingly handsome gentleman with a leonine mane of blond hair and sharp blue eyes. "Lucas is the detective."

"You've got to remember," Lucas Kendrick told the lawyer in his curiously compelling voice, "that the boss didn't send for us. Zach did. And though I've been here only a day, I agree with him. There's something very fishy going on."

"Well, what?"

Zach, never stirring from a deep chair where he somewhat grimly contemplated the remainder of the brandy in his glass, told the newly arrived lawyer everything that had happened up until that day, finishing with, "Lucas has been following the lady; he'll tell you the rest."

The chief investigator for Josh's empire took up the story. "I asked questions about her at the apartment building where the manager denied to Josh that lady lived there; she made the same denial to me. Claimed the place was empty. Then I checked out the other apartment, and it *is* leased to Travers, not sublet. The staff wouldn't talk.

"She left the penthouse this morning, did a quick-change routine in a garage, and met a man at a museum. If I hadn't known to look for the Pinto, I would have missed her, because she looked that different. It was definitely a prearranged meeting, maybe for some kind of exchange of information. I couldn't go into the room to overhear them. I would have been too obvious; the room was empty except for them."

Rafferty's normally humorous face was sober, as was his voice. "And then?"

"Then she returned to the garage, changed back to her glamorous self, and went back to the penthouse." He shook his head, frowning. "I managed to find a talkative maid in the cleaning service for the building—not easy, believe me. Their security is pretty tight. But the maid said Raven Anderson is very quietly known as the Ice Maiden. She's been there only a few weeks. None of the staff believes she's Travers's mistress; they think he'd have more luck with a glacier."

"And domestic help usually knows that kind of thing," Rafferty observed almost to himself.

"Damn right they do." Lucas sighed. "So it looks like the boss was right about that, anyway."

Zach stirred a bit and looked at the other two. "Maybe he's right about the rest. When he came out of the penthouse the other night, he *believed* her. Somehow, she'd convinced him. And we all know how many women have tried to con Josh in one way or another through the years. He's nobody's fool. I think he's right about her background being fabricated."

Rafferty looked at him sharply. "Because Josh believes in her? Or was there something that finally turned up in her background? You said it checked out."

"Oh, it did." Zach nodded morosely. "On the surface. We dug deeper, and it checked out. Then we kept digging—and a funny thing is happening."

"Don't keep us in suspense," Josh drawled from the doorway.

The three men watched as he came out of his bedroom and moved to lean against the desk. None of them got to their feet, but only because Josh disliked formality. Besides, their respect for Josh needed no outward signs to be apparent.

Rafferty, the newest arrival, blinked when he saw his friend and employer of several years. Josh had lost weight, he realized, and there was something different in his eyes, something almost haunted. "Hello, Josh."

"Rafferty." Josh smiled a little. "Come to keep me out of jail, or what?"

"You been ignoring your parking tickets?"

"No."

"Well, then, I'm just here as an advisor. I think."
He looked at Zach, who nodded.

"I thought he should be here, Josh. Things are
beginning to look damn complicated."

Josh crossed his arms over his chest and laughed
faintly with no humor. "I might have known I
couldn't even conduct a private courtship without
trouble of some kind." His life was a public one,
and Josh had learned over the years that nothing
could be simple for him. Then he shot Rafferty a
quick look. "In case they didn't convince you, that
dossier on Raven is a bundle of lies—or some
awful mistake."

"They convinced me."

"Fine." Josh looked at Zach. "So what's funny?"

"Well, as I said, we dug deeper. And all of a
sudden, people aren't talking to us. With a ven-
geance. And Lucas's contact in the intelligence
community just closed down tight as a drum."

"I couldn't get the time of day from him," the
investigator confirmed. "It smells, Josh."

Josh, who knew quite a bit himself about intelligence games, frowned. "A coverup?"

"No, just dead silence. And my instincts are
yelling that we're about to be warned off. Somebody doesn't want us digging into Raven Anderson's background."

"Travers?"

"The odor doesn't drift from that direction. Federal, I'd say."

Josh thought of the keen intelligence in violet
eyes. "You think it's possible she might be an
operative for one of the agencies?"

"It's possible. It's also *possible*," Lucas said
evenly, "that they've got an eye on her and don't

want us mucking around and screwing up their gameplan."

"No."

Lucas slid a glance toward Zach, then said very softly, "I lifted a few prints off the car this morning. They match the file."

"The file's fabricated. I don't know why, but I know it's fake." Utter certainty.

Glances were exchanged between the security man, the attorney, and the investigator and a decision silently reached and affirmed among the three of them.

"All right," Zach said. "We go from there. And working from that premise, Josh, I say we back off. Now."

"I agree," Rafferty said, and Lucas nodded.

It took Josh only a moment to realize why the suggestion had been made, and he went cold all over. He should have seen it, *would* have seen it except that he'd been too involved, too bent on finding out what was going on.

"If we keep digging—" he murmured, breaking off.

Rafferty spoke quietly. "If she's undercover—the only logical explanation for a fabricated background like hers—and we work like hell to expose that cover as a fake, we could put her in very great danger. Especially with a man like Leon Travers involved. Whatever's going on, he's at the hub of it."

"Look at it this way," Lucas said. "It's been rumored for years that Travers is very heavily into white slavery, but nobody's been able to pin a thing on him. Now, within the last few weeks, a lady enters his life. A lady with a rock-solid criminal background and a CIA report that she represents international interests in that area. Now, if that background and that report are false, then there's only one good reason for it. I think somebody's setting Travers up. It's the only thing that makes sense."

"And if we poke our noses in . . ." Rafferty murmured.

"He could turn on Raven," Josh murmured, his face gray, fear for her twisting his guts and sending ice through his veins. "Smell a set-up and decide to cover his tracks."

Josh had seen the results of evil minds at work far too many times in his life, and the thought of Raven trapped unsuspectingly, at the mercy of one such as Travers, filled him with agony. There were so many things a brutal man could do to a woman, so many ways to hurt her, scar her inside and out for life . . . even to the point where death would be a welcome release.

"You're at risk too," Zach said, going on even when Josh gestured dismissively. "Travers has his own intelligence network, and from all reports it's damned good. We've taken the usual precautions in checking into her background, but we didn't know what we were up against. If Travers got suspicious, he'd find out quick enough that you're behind it. And he knows damned well who you are, Josh. He knows you've helped law enforcement and intelligence agencies before, and he knows how you feel about criminal activities on his grand scale. He could decide to go after you."

"I would, in his place," Lucas said flatly. "You're more than just a threat to him, Josh. You're a deadly danger. You have very powerful friends, and you could make a hell of a lot of trouble for him if you decided to."

It was Rafferty who added the clincher. "And if Travers should discover that your interest in Raven is personal, he'll have a lever to use against you."

"I have to see Raven," Josh said hoarsely, reaching for the phone. "Warn her. I have to tell her what I've done—"

"What we've done," Zach said.

Across town in a shabby apartment building, and roughly an hour before Josh and his lieutenants had reached their conclusions, Kelsey hunched forward, staring at a computer screen. His eyes widened as information scrolled past for endless moments, then he swore softly and reached for the telephone.

"Hello?" a cool voice answered.

"Is Susan there?" Kelsey asked cheerfully.

"You have the wrong number," the cultured voice of Raven told him.

"Sorry." He hung up, knowing that this had been as good a time as any to use their emergency, one-time-only code; he had to see Raven, and quickly.

He reviewed the information his computer offered, shaking his head unconsciously. Damn. Double damn. How in *hell* were they going to deal with this mess? Trust Raven to go and fall in love with the one man who could ruin everything!

It was only a matter of time, he thought, until Travers found out from his intelligence network that Joshua Long had been digging into Raven's background.

The Joshua Long, dammit, known far and wide as an extremely brilliant, powerful, wealthy . . . and *honest* man.

What could they do? Bluster it out, find some reason for Long's interest in Raven that wouldn't send Travers berserk? Recruit Long and somehow make the situation reasonable and no threat to Travers? Push up the timetable and trust to blind luck that they'd have the job done before Travers knew anything at all?

Kelsey made a second call, scrambling it at his end and routing it so that it would take endless time to trace.

He needed advice from the top.

Four

All four men jumped in surprise when the door of the suite was suddenly assaulted by clearly angry fists. Absolutely furious fists. Zach, who was nearest, went to peer cautiously through the peephole, then swore audibly in a surprised tone and quickly opened the door. A second later, he found himself shoved rather unceremoniously aside to allow the entrance of what was obviously an avenging fury.

"Out of my way!"

Josh, who had been chain-smoking and listening to the endless ringing in his ear, dropped the receiver home, stubbed out his latest cigarette, and rose to his feet swiftly. "Raven!"

Flashing violet eyes seared past a lawyer and an investigator, both climbing to their feet, and fixed on Josh. "You!" She advanced on him. "Do you know what you've done? Do you have any *idea* what you've done? I ought to—"

Heedless of both her anger and the fascinated

presence of his lieutenants, Josh yanked her somewhat roughly into his arms and kissed her thoroughly, his relief almost overpowering. She was
safe. For now, at least, she was safe.

For an instant, Raven melted against him, but
then anger resurfaced and she fought free of him.
"No, dammit! *Now* I know why you're so good at
this! You're a damned playboy, you've been prac-
ticing for *years*!"

Varied deep tones of laughter jerked her attention away from Josh, and she whirled to stare
at the three men she'd barely noticed until then.
"Who the hell are you?" she snarled. In her
present mood she would have made the same
furious demand of the devil if he'd stood before
her breathing fire and complete with horns and
pitchfork.

Josh rested his hip on the edge of his desk
and grinned despite himself. This new aspect of
Raven's personality intrigued him, and he eyed
her as he murmured introductions.

Hands on her hips, magnificent eyes blazing,
Raven turned her attention to a suddenly uncomfortable Lucas. "*You* asked questions at my
apartment," she accused him. "And you followed
me; I thought I'd lost you."

"I've had a lot of practice," Lucas muttered, more
than a little annoyed with himself for having been
spotted.

"So have I," she retorted, plainly angry. "And at
more than losing a tail; follow me again and you'll
find out a few other things I've had practice at. I
can promise you they're *painful*."

Settling his bulk back into a chair, Zach said,

"If the jury were still out, I guess that'd bring it in quick enough. We were right, Josh."

Raven was still too angry to guard her tongue, not in the least because finding that Josh Long actually *did* have a kingdom, an empire, really, had shaken her more than a little. She skewered the big security chief with a glare. "Jury? You'd all be *hung* for what you've done! And I'd hold the damned rope! Months—*months!*—of work down the drain because lover boy here couldn't resist throwing his weight around!"

Willingly, Josh drew the inevitable explosion to himself rather than to his lieutenants; he was nothing if not fair, and it had been his fault that they'd probed into her background. He said, "If you'd been honest with me—"

Raven turned to give him a look that should have shriveled him on the spot. "I didn't know you from Adam's housecat," she snapped, ignoring a choke of laughter from behind her. "And I don't shoot my mouth off every chance I get!" Belatedly realizing that in fact she was doing just that, Raven fell silent and continued to glare at him.

Josh looked past her at his friends. "Would you excuse us?"

Rafferty, the last out the door, glanced back to say solemnly, "Maybe I should stay, Josh. You might need somebody to uphold your rights."

Josh lifted an eyebrow at him, holding on to his dignity as much as possible after having been violently labeled a playboy and "lover boy" in front of his men. Rafferty laughed and closed the door softly as he left.

Looking at Raven and fighting the desire to

take her back into his arms, Josh said quietly, "I was trying to reach you just now before you came in." He nodded toward his absent friends. "They made me realize what I'd done. I'm sorry, Raven. I wasn't thinking. That fabricated dossier on you just . . . I almost went out of my mind."

Raven turned abruptly and walked to the window, staring out. When Kelsey had summoned her with their emergency code, she hadn't even bothered to assume a disguise; she had simply switched cars and taken pains to make certain she wasn't followed. And since Leon was at a board meeting, she'd felt reasonably safe in charging over here to confront Josh.

She was dressed as she'd been when Kelsey called, in a white silk dress that clung lovingly to her breasts and waist before flowing out in a full skirt to brush her knees. And she was wearing the makeup for her role, nothing heavy, but a suggestion of catlike mystery slanted her eyes due to soft shadowing, and the planes of her face, expertly contoured, seemed sharpened, curiously exotic.

Very softly, Josh said, "I could guess the role you're playing even without the file on you. A woman of mystery, seductive but never seduced. Igniting fire, but never burning herself. Spinning the threads of a web that never catches her." Abruptly and on a rueful note, he added, "You should meet my sister."

Raven ignored the apparent non sequitur. Instead, she thought of his summation of her role, and almost laughed. Judging by the performance she just enacted for his men, she wasn't as good an actress as Josh seemed to think. Damn him for making her lose control, she thought, but there was no venom in the reflection, not even anger.

"Raven—"

"Why couldn't you listen to me," she asked, striving to keep her voice even. "Why did you have to probe?"

"It was too late to stop," he answered soberly. "We had already been digging into your background. And after I left you at the penthouse, I was so afraid you were in over your head, so afraid you'd get hurt."

"I was perfectly safe." She looked at him. "Then."

Josh drew a deep breath and let it out slowly. "Raven, I'd give everything I have to take back all the probing, to get you out of the danger I've put you in." She was, he thought dimly, looking at him rather oddly.

"Tell me something," Raven requested. "Just what is it you believe I'm involved in?"

He didn't hesitate. "I believe you're working with or for someone who wants to put Leon Travers behind bars for good. Probably on charges relating to white slavery."

She never changed expression; her professional mask was in place now. "I see. Well, Kelsey seemed to be convinced you'd figure it out quickly."

"Kelsey?"

"My partner."

Questions leaped to Josh's mind, but he held them back. He'd done enough damage already with his questions. "It was the only thing that made sense," he said. "Zach turned up that file on you pretty quickly and I—couldn't believe it. You were gone, out of reach; all I had was that damned file burning itself into my brain. I had to disprove it. That's why I went to the penthouse."

"You thought I was Leon Travers's mistress."

"No," he said quickly. "I knew there had to be a reason, an explanation—"

Raven laughed, a sound with no amusement. Her eyes, briefly, were hard with remembered pain. "That wasn't the impression you gave me in the penthouse."

He took a step toward her, then halted as she stiffened visibly. "Raven, please try to understand. I had fallen in love for the first time in my life with a wonderful, beautiful woman with laughing eyes. All I knew was that I loved her. And then, with no time granted to get closer to her, she's gone. And in front of me is a file, and a picture, and the certainty that she's staying in Travers's penthouse."

"You believed it." She knew she wasn't being fair, knew all too well the evidence had been damning. But the pain was still in her and she couldn't be professional about it.

He took another step, his eyes direct and steady, his face a little pale. "No. I was half out of my mind, but no matter how wild I was, I couldn't believe it of you. That's why I kept digging, Raven. That's why I couldn't let it alone."

"I asked you to trust me."

"I did. But I was afraid for you."

With an effort that broke something inside of her, Raven turned her eyes from him and stared out the window. She could literally feel his tension, his intense drive to convince her. The peculiar empathy hardly surprised her, since it was familiar by now, but she did wonder vaguely how a man could look as calm as Josh usually did while hiding the powerful emotions she could feel emanating from him.

But, then, wasn't she hiding her own emotions? The thought had barely occurred when Raven felt the sting of tears, and knew her own surface control was being stripped away. Damn the man! He had destroyed years of training and experience. Fiercely, she blinked away the tears.

"Raven."

His voice was near, too near, and she moved almost convulsively to escape it. But his hands fell on her shoulders and she was turned to face him. And it was too much, just suddenly too much. She had to *do* something. Those years of training and experience exploded within her, and Raven reacted as if some murderous fiend had laid hands upon her.

With blinding speed and sharp-honed reflexes, she twisted in an expert move that not twenty people in the entire world would have been able to match or counter. In theory—and, until now, in practice—her attacker would have been on the floor, completely unconscious.

Instead, Raven's move was countered with equally blinding speed, even with the handicap of his determination not to hurt her. Breathless and shaking, she looked up into his eyes, both her wrists caught at the small of her back and her body locked helplessly against his. He held her trapped. The deep V neckline of her dress had shifted during her violent movement so that one shoulder had slipped downward, and she said absolutely nothing as Josh lifted his free hand to gently smooth the white silk back into place.

Gazing into violet eyes that were both angry and stunned, he said softly, "You've been well taught. But so have I."

Her voice was husky. "There aren't twenty people in the world who could counter that defense."

"Twenty-two. My sister and I were taught secretly."

She was dizzily conscious of the feeling of her breasts pressed against his hard chest, of his thighs against her own. But she held her voice steady. "Why secretly?"

The hand at her shoulder lifted to gently brush back a strand of her long hair, and his eyes followed the movement fleetingly until his hand lay against her neck warmly. "My stepfather thought it best. If no one knew my sister and I could defend ourselves, we had an ace up our sleeves."

Raven swallowed, aware suddenly of throbbing desire; she wasn't sure if it was hers or his. It didn't matter. "Why was it necessary? Because you were wealthy?"

"Partly." His voice had deepened, grown husky. "But also because my stepfather is Stuart Jameson."

Her eyes widened; she might not have been familiar with the social and business scene, but the top scientific circles held no faces that would have been strange to her. "I heard him lecture years ago. He talked to us about worst-case scenarios; he said you always had to plan for the worst, and know what you'd do if it happened."

Josh nodded slowly, his eyes now fixed on her lips. "He told Serena and me the same thing from the time we were very young."

Raven remembered something else then, and

her breath caught in her throat. "His wife . . . she was killed by accident, because someone was trying to get to him."

His eyes darkening, Josh nodded again. "My mother."

She was scarcely aware that he'd released her wrists, and wasn't conscious of her action when she lifted her arms and slid them around his waist. Her heart was aching suddenly. "Your mother . . . Oh, Josh, I'm sorry."

"It was a long time ago." Still, there was a thread of grief in his voice. "But I haven't forgotten Stuart's lessons. You see, Raven, when I realized what I'd done, and what you were involved in, those years of lessons took control. I saw so clearly what Travers could do to you. All the ways he could hurt you." He drew a deep breath unsteadily.

"I didn't realize . . ."

In a peculiarly conversational tone far more chilling than any outburst would have been, Josh said, "I would have killed him, you know. If you hadn't walked in, I would have gone after him. I just couldn't take the chance he wouldn't turn on you."

"Josh—"

His hand tangled in her long hair, and Josh bent his head, taking her mouth fiercely. Raven's lips parted instantly, allowing the slow probing of his tongue, feeling that stark caress ignite a curl of fire deep inside her.

And there was something else deep inside her, something both excited and astonished. Never in her life had a man's touch affected her like this, ignited fire so swiftly and completely. She had known she loved him, but not even that knowledge had prepared her for this instantaneous explosion of all her senses, this mindless need to belong to him.

The past years had been filled with too much reality for Raven to indulge in fantasies, but her mind conjured images now, inspired by the demands of her body. She could see him naked and powerful in his desire, his muscled body sleek and strong and primitive. And her own body ached hollowly, insistently, demanding his strength to fill the emptiness.

Her soft moan was lost in his mouth as she felt him move against her, the thin barriers of her silk dress and his clothing flimsy things easily penetrated by the heat and demand of their bodies. The curl of fire in her belly became molten, flowing through her veins until she was burning from head to foot.

The restless heat made her move unconsciously against him, instinctively seeking relief from the growing tension, her nails digging into his back. And even though a distant, constantly guarded part of her mind was aware of voices and activity in the room around them, she was gloriously unconcerned by it.

"Uh . . . Josh?"

Josh lifted his head, staring down into her dazed eyes. "Get out of here, Zach," he murmured hoarsely, his fixed gaze drifting downward to absorb the faintly swollen red lips that were parted and seemed mutely to beg for another kiss. And he wanted to oblige. Dear Lord, how he wanted to oblige!

"I'd love to," Zach muttered, apparently having some trouble with his voice. "Believe me, I'd love to. But we have a visitor, and he seems determined to talk to you."

"Tell him to go to hell," Josh said absently, still staring at Raven's upturned face. The eyeshadow that was a part of her role, he thought, certainly gave her the enigmatic gaze of a feline. But a woman looked out of those violet eyes, and every male instinct he could lay claim to urged him to carry her away somewhere and lock out the world.

"Mind if I get there in my own good time?" a new voice inquired dryly.

Josh felt Raven stiffen slowly in his arms, her eyes clearing of desire as though a cool breeze had blown through her, and he was surprised to see her wince slightly as she turned her head to look at the visitor, her expression rueful. She didn't disentangle herself from the embrace, but it was obvious that something had distracted her from passion.

Josh didn't bother to look; it was enough that someone had disturbed his Raven. "Whoever you are, leave!"

"No," the visitor returned with wonderful simplicity.

In a giddy moment, torn between the demands of his body and an innate sense of humor, Josh was tempted to roar, "Off with his head!" Not that he did, of course. Raven's talk of princes and his own of kingdoms—not to mention the frustrated throbbing of his desire—had merely addled his wits, he decided.

"Hello, Hagen," Raven said in a soft, depressed tone.

"Raven. Fancy meeting you here." The man's voice was very gentle.

She cleared her throat rather oddly, an absurdly guilty expression flickering in her eyes. Josh, annoyed, decided that the visitor had better say what he'd come for and then leave promptly since he was so clearly upsetting Raven.

Accordingly, Josh prepared to deal with the situation. And in his state of mind, he dealt wonderfully. He kept an arm around Raven while he retreated behind his desk, then sat down and pulled her onto his lap.

"Josh . . ." she said in a voice hovering somewhere between amusement and horror. Though he didn't know it, she was remembering an inebriated suitor who had courted her cheerfully and humorously in a crowded tavern without giving a damn that he was wearing his heart on his sleeve. And she thought she loved him more in this moment than ever before.

With a lap full of Raven, it was difficult for Josh to glare at anyone at all, but he gave it his best shot and turned an irritated gaze to the visitor. What he saw gained the visitor no points at all.

"Hagen" was a rotund little man dwarfed by all three of Josh's lieutenants as they stood around him in a semi-circle. He couldn't have been much more than five four, and the three-piece business suit he wore could have used the services of a good tailor; it was straining at the seams and stretched almost indecently over an unashamed paunch. The man had the face of a cherub, complete with fat rosy cheeks and small twinkling eyes. And on his round head reposed a battered fedora that a skid-row bum would have chucked into the garbage.

Appalled by this image, Josh closed his eyes

briefly and drew Raven a reassuring inch closer.
"Out with it," he directed impatiently. "What do
you want?"

Hagen removed his hat and twirled it between
his pudgy hands in a ridiculous gesture. "Just a
moment of your time, Mr. Long."

"Whatever you're selling, I don't want any." Josh
was mildly disappointed in his security chief because this character had somehow managed to
hoodwink Zach into letting him enter the suite.
"Out."

Raven made an oddly choked little sound and
whispered, "Josh, you don't understand—"

Rafferty unintentionally cut her off. "Josh, I
think you'd better listen to him. He said he was—"

It was Hagen's turn to interrupt. And he did, in
a suddenly soft and steely voice. "Call your stepfather, Mr. Long. Tell him my name."

Josh's gaze sharpened as he stared at Hagen.
Those twinkling little eyes, he realized, were so
vivid not because of humor but because of keen
intelligence. And he also realized belatedly that
Raven knew this man, and respected him.

"Call Stuart Jameson," Hagen said, and it was
not—quite—a command.

Josh reached out a hand to pull the phone
nearer, taking his eyes off Hagen only when it
became necessary to punch out the number. Then
he returned his unreadable gaze to the strange
visitor.

Raven, sitting still and silent in his lap, listened
to his end of the conversation only vaguely. Her
present position, not to mention the embrace Hagen had walked in on, left her at something of a
disadvantage, but she couldn't seem to summon

the strength to defend herself. Not that any defense would have sufficed for Hagen.

Josh had reached his stepfather quickly and just as quickly named Hagen and described him somewhat unflatteringly. Then he fell silent, and only Raven could hear the long and steady response from the receiver; to her it was little more than sound, and she didn't bother to try to listen harder. She knew what was being said.

When Josh finally cradled the receiver, he hadn't changed expression. But his eyes were speculative, and his voice was, if not friendly, then certainly more polite than before. "All right, Mr. Hagen, now I know who you are. Have a seat and tell me what you're doing here."

Hagen accepted the brusque invitation, making his way to a chair near the desk. "You're cleared to hear what I have to say," he said. "What about your men?"

"Them too. I don't keep secrets from them." Josh glanced at Raven, and sudden humor lit his eyes. "None at all, in fact."

Raven, abruptly aware of what he meant, glanced at the three big men now arranging themselves on the couch and chairs, and her gaze skittered away. Precious few secrets, she thought wryly, conscious of just how much these men knew.

Hagen accepted Josh's assurances and glanced at each of his three men briefly before focusing those bright little eyes on Josh. He splendidly ignored Raven's position. "Since you now know who I am, you must also realize that I'm Raven's, uh, boss."

"Yes."

"I trust," Hagen said gently, "you didn't know

that before you blundered in and possibly ruined months of work, Mr. Long."

Josh's eyes hardened. "No."

Hagen sighed a bit, apparently at the vagaries of fate. "No, of course not. And Raven, professional though she certainly is, had no idea that in one half of her double life she was becoming involved with a man who could destroy the other half." He brooded on that for a moment, adding to himself, "I must make certain that never happens again. Operatives should be familiar with important people outside their own circle of interest."

Josh looked at Raven. "Your circle of interest?"

Since her chief's presence here was tacit permission to speak, Raven did. "I specialize in kidnappings and the white slave trade," she explained, trying very hard to forget she was sitting in his lap. "The kidnappings are usually much simpler, because ransom demands are made; in white slavery, the girls just disappear."

Josh had removed his interest from Hagen, and was in no hurry to return it. He continued to gaze at Raven, and tried to forget she was in his lap; it had, he remembered, seemed like a good idea at the time, but it was infinitely distracting now. "I see. How long have you been involved in this kind of work?"

"Actively, five years. Training before that."

Five years on the dark side of life . . . Josh shook his head. "Why?" he asked her.

Raven didn't need the question elaborated; she'd asked it herself often enough. "The usual reasons, I guess. Excitement, danger, adventure. And . . . I wanted to do something to help."

Very quietly, Hagen said, "Tell him, Raven."

She turned her head to look at the deceptively foolish-looking man, then back at Josh. Her expression was strained. "I had a sister," she said simply. "An older sister. My senior year in college, my sister went on a vacation with some friends. She never came back."

Josh felt a slow, heavy pain roll inside him. For the first time, he saw a faint shadow in her eyes, and her hurt was his. "Was she . . ."

"I found her." Raven's voice was soft and toneless. "When she disappeared, I spent a year searching for her. That was when Hagen contacted me, and offered to train me; I was having no luck at all in finding my sister, but I was making a lot of noise."

"And I heard it," Hagen interjected.

Josh kept his eyes on Raven's immobile face, waiting for the blow, very sure it would be just that.

"I took the training, and learned where to look and what to look for. But she'd been missing so long. It was sheer luck that I found her." Raven's soft voice was the only sound in the room. "She . . . hadn't been as lucky as some girls are. The first man to . . . to buy her had tired of her quickly and sold her. It was downhill after that. I found her in the Middle East. In a whorehouse."

Josh gritted his teeth to keep from groaning aloud, and his arms instinctively drew her closer. Painted in neon in his mind was the accusation he had all but made, and her soft, toneless response. *I'm not a whore.* No wonder she had looked so shattered!

Raven was going on. "They'd kept her strung out on drugs, and she was sick. . . . She never recognized me. And didn't live long enough to come home."

"Raven . . ." It was no more than a whisper.

She looked at him for a moment, her eyes clearing slowly of shadows, then managed a smile. "I guess that's the real reason I kept the job."

Hagen began talking quietly, obviously deciding that it was time to reveal exactly what Raven was involved in now. "We've known for years that Leon Travers was involved in white slavery, but couldn't trace it to him personally. He's protected by layers and layers of blind, deaf, and mute employees who know only too well that to betray him means death."

Josh, still hurting for Raven, forced himself to pay attention. "Then what makes you think you can pin it on him now?"

"He made a mistake. Or, perhaps, to put it more accurately, someone in his organization did. A few weeks ago, two young girls were abducted three blocks away from their home in Virginia. They are seventeen, and extraordinarily beautiful. Twins. A novelty . . . a novelty that would command a high price from some."

Josh nodded, and made a guess. "And special in another way?"

Hagen looked approving. "Stuart always said you were sharp. Yes, indeed, they are special girls. They were raised quietly, out of public view to allow them privacy, but they happen to be the daughters of a very important man. Within hours, he had notified the proper authority—me—that his daughters were missing. And because of his quickness, we were able to get a lead almost immediately.

"We allowed no publicity of the disappearance, and worked very quietly. Within days we had traced the girls to California, and then the general area of Los Angeles. There had been no ransom demand, so we felt strongly that whoever had taken the girls meant to make their money in another way. But we didn't know who had planned the snatch. There are far more of these prostitution rings than the average person would believe existed.

"It was at that point, when, admittedly, we had lost the girls, that we had a stroke of sheer luck. One of my operatives was conducting some strictly routine surveillance on Travers and saw him briefly visit a very respectable house in a suburban neighborhood. The operative was only mildly suspicious, until one of those bright girls managed to toss her expensive gold bracelet out a window. He caught no more than a glimpse of the girl, but that bracelet was as good as a signature."

Josh felt a slow anger building within him. It was fueled by his extensive experience with covert operations. He hated the practice of delaying the rescue of victims in order to capture "important" criminals. "Why didn't you move?" he demanded. "Get them out of there?"

Hagen smiled thinly, understanding the source of the younger man's anger. "We did move, Mr. Long. Within two hours, which was how long it took us to get a team out there to deal with the armed guards my operative saw. But the girls were gone. And the operative left there had disappeared as well."

Josh nodded, half in apology. "I see. The trail was cold again. Except for Travers."

"Except for Travers." If Hagen accepted the tacit apology, he didn't say so. "By that time, we had accumulated a considerable file on Travers. And we had evidence to support our belief that he had a network of safe houses so that his girls could be moved frequently. Never the same house twice, and never for more than a day or so in any place. We were also certain that the girls were kept in the area for at least two months while the details of their sale were being worked out. So we had that long to find them."

Josh, thinking of what those girls were probably going through, stirred restlessly. "Those poor kids. Held prisoner, guarded, abused—" He broke off as he realized that Hagen was looking steadily at Raven. He followed the other man's gaze, and she responded to his worry.

"No, not abused. Decent food, no drugs except for mild sedatives. And no rape." Wryly, she explained, "High-priced slavery rings don't damage their merchandise. Virginity also commands a high price, and some customers demand a doctor's certificate to attest to it."

She sounded so certain, and Josh felt a chill. "Raven . . . how do you know?" Her gaze avoided his, moving instead to Hagen and looking at him in what seemed a pleading manner. Clearly, she didn't want to answer Josh's question.

Hagen did. "Twice in the past three years," he said quietly, "Raven has been 'kidnapped' into white slavery. She went the entire route, from the initial snatch to the customer who . . . bought her." He must have seen the savagery in the stare Josh sent his way, because he explained probably more than he wanted to or meant to. "We were with her every step of the way, of course. She was never in any more danger than she would have been in crossing a street."

For the first time, one of Josh's lieutenants spoke. It was Zach, and his voice was harsh. "Right. And the sun rises in the West. Why don't you tell us a few fairy tales?"

Raven looked at the big security chief in surprise at the suppressed violence of his reaction, but Hagen smiled. "It was her decision—her request, in fact. And she wasn't harmed. Thanks to her work, we were able to break both slavery rings; before, we couldn't touch them."

Josh didn't want to think of Raven in such situations, even if they had apparently ended safely. He got the conversation back on track. "Okay, so the girls are reasonably safe. Travers was your only lead. Then what?"

Hagen nodded. "We had spent a considerable amount of time and gone to a lot of trouble to fabricate a foolproof background for an international 'buyer' in the event of need. And this was the situation we had planned for. I brought Raven back—"

"From where?" Josh interrupted, distracted again.

Hagen grimaced faintly at the digression, but answered. "Hong Kong."

Josh looked at Raven, who showed the first flash of humor in quite some time. In what seemed like magic, and by merely lowering her eyelids and apparently *thinking* Oriental, she suddenly looked distinctly Oriental. "It's amazing what you can get away with if you're wearing a kimono," she murmured.

Josh thought his mouth was open, and hastily closed it as his friends burst out laughing. Bemused, he looked back at Hagen. "Obviously, you brought her back from Hong Kong. And then?"

"We made the necessary alterations to our fabricated background: Raven's prints, photograph, and so on. Then we circulated rumors in the correct quarters and waited a couple of days for interest to stir. Travers, as expected, stirred. We set Raven up in a ridiculously expensive suite in the best hotel in the city—and he came calling almost immediately."

Josh was frowning, the moment of humor forgotten. "Travers is paranoid; it's common knowledge. What made you so certain he'd accept Raven so quickly?"

The lost humor was hovering in Hagen's eyes. "A reason I believe you'll appreciate, Mr. Long. You see, Travers, like all men, has his weaknesses. And his greatest weakness of all is twofold. First, quixotic though it sounds and difficult as it is to believe, he possesses a sincere liking for women. It's his blind spot in a very real sense. He's suspicious of every man on earth, but never women. The only really surprising thing is that no one's used it against him. Until I decided to."

Josh was still frowning, but not because he doubted Hagen's conclusions. He had, in fact, heard something along the same lines himself. "Are you saying," he demanded, "that Raven isn't in danger from him?"

"No. Oh, no—that would be too easy, wouldn't it? But his trust is easily won by women, comparatively speaking. And easily destroyed in the specific, although never in the abstract; if he stops trusting one woman, he doesn't stop trusting them all. No, Raven could easily be in danger if she lost the trust she's been at some pains to build with him."

Josh absorbed those words. Then, accepting them, he felt the fear roll through him again at the thought of the danger he had placed her in. "All right. You said his weakness was twofold?"

"Exactly. And that was another reason to recall Raven." Hagen was smiling broadly now. "You see, Mr. Long, Travers has a weakness for women. And an absolute obsession for beautiful brunettes."

Five

Ironic though it certainly was, Josh had no difficulty in accepting that. He sighed a little and
looked at Raven, resisting the nearly overpowering urge to kiss her and the hell with watching
eyes. Then he looked at Hagen. "I see."

"He treats me like a lady," Raven offered. "Even
though he *knows* . . . well, what I'm supposed to
be. He's never even made a pass. I've had more
trouble with Theodore than Leon."

"Who's Theodore?" Josh asked.

Unconsciously, Raven toyed with the fingers lying
warmly across her silk-covered thigh. "*What's* Theodore is more like it," she said dryly. "He's some
kind of assistant to Leon, but the man is totally
inept. And whenever Leon isn't nearby, Theodore
makes passes right and left." Parenthetically, she
added, "He has clammy hands."

She wondered why she wasn't experiencing a
loss of dignity in sitting on Josh's lap with four
men watching, but felt as gloriously unconcerned

as she had when those same four men had interrupted earlier. It didn't seem to matter.

Even with the deadly seriousness of what they were discussing, Josh was having a very nearly impossible time concentrating on the matter at hand. He had an instant surge of anger when he heard that anyone made unwelcome passes at Raven, but the emotion was fleeting due to her unconcern; obviously, she could handle Theodore. Remembering her defensive move earlier, Josh thought she could handle most men.

He glanced down to watch her fingers toying with his, vaguely glad that the other men could see nothing because of the desk. Also vaguely, he wondered how long he could continue to sit tamely with Raven in his lap and not turn rabid.

Hagen spoke into the silence. "So, you see, we have at least two strong points in our favor. But when Travers discovers, as he most certainly will, that Joshua Long has been thoroughly checking Raven's background, he's not going to smell a romance. He's going to smell a trap."

Josh forced all his attention on Hagen, helped by the very real danger Raven was facing. With reluctant logic, he said, "And you can't pull her out. There isn't enough time to bring another operative in to win his trust, is there?"

"No."

Josh stirred restlessly, then went still as his body reacted violently. He cleared his throat and tried to think. "What, then? You must have a plan."

"That depends on you." Hagen was smiling faintly. "I have a plan of sorts. I think it will work.

Don't forget, I've accumulated information on Travers for years. I've observed him in almost every conceivable situation. I've crawled in and out of his head so many times, I know how he thinks. And I believe we can set the stage so that he will instantly and quite naturally accept your abrupt presence in Raven's life as no threat at all."

"Well? What's the plan?"

Glancing at the three men sitting near him, Hagen murmured, "The fewer people who know about this . . ."

Mildly, Zach said, "We aren't known for our lack of discretion."

Josh gave Hagen a level look. "The plan."

Apparently convinced that Josh's lieutenants were trustworthy, Hagen smiled benignly at Josh. "How willing are you to make a public fool of yourself?"

"Where would you like to have dinner, my dear?"

Back in her ice-maiden persona, Raven allowed her fingertips to rest lightly on Leon Travers's arm as they left the elevator. "I'll leave it to you." As always, her voice was cool and cultured, her expression detached; both spoke volumes for her acting ability, since she was tense and anxious. What if something went wrong?

And, almost immediately, something did.

Theodore scurried across the lobby toward them, a rabbit pursued by imaginary hounds, and hailed his employer and relative nervously. "Leon, I can't find that contract!"

Travers stopped walking and stared at the younger man, the expression in his gray eyes unreadable. "We won't need it until tomorrow, Theodore," he reminded him in a gentle tone that didn't quite hide annoyance.

Theodore blinked rapidly. "I know, but—"

"Tomorrow, Theodore."

Raven, detached, gazed into the middle distance and idly considered telling Travers that his rabbity relation had clammy hands with a habit of wandering, but discarded the notion. She was getting giddy with tension, she knew, and resisted an urge to glance at her watch.

"But, Leon—" Theodore bleated, only to be interrupted by a roar from the building's front entrance.

"Travers!"

Theodore yelped in panic and leaped behind a marble column, his face shocked and frightened. But he quickly found out that no one was bothering with him.

Josh Long pushed his way past a startled doorman and strode toward the couple near the elevator, his face livid with anger and his eyes flashing dangerously. Behind him, also pushing past the doorman, came his obviously worried lieutenants, Rafferty and Lucas, both clearly bent on stopping their employer from doing something rash.

Travers never moved, but Raven felt him stiffen as Josh neared, not relaxing even when the other two men caught Josh in firm hands and halted his headlong rush.

"It'll look more impressive," Hagen had said, "if it takes both of them to hold you. Not him, though." A nod toward Zach. "Overkill. He could hold back an army."

America's most popular, most compelling romance novels...

Here, at last...love stories that really involve you! Fresh, finely crafted novels with story lines so believable you'll feel you're actually living them! Characters you can relate to...exciting places to visit...unexpected plot twists...all in all, exciting romances that satisfy your mind and delight your heart.

Now you can be sure you'll never, ever miss a single Loveswept title by enrolling in our special reader's home delivery service. A service that will bring all four new Loveswept romances published every month into your home—and deliver them to you before they appear in the bookstores!

Examine 4 Loveswept Novels for

15 days FREE!

(SEE OTHER SIDE FOR DETAILS)

Postage will be paid by addressee

Loveswept

Bantam Books
P.O. Box 985
Hicksville, NY 11802

BUSINESS REPLY MAIL

FIRST-CLASS MAIL   PERMIT NO. 2456   HICKSVILLE, NY

NO POSTAGE
NECESSARY
IF MAILED
IN THE
UNITED STATES

"I don't believe we've met," Travers offered in a civilized tone, for all the world as if they had encountered each other at a social function.

"Get your hands off her!" Josh sent him a look that should have nailed him to the wall. "You *bastard*!" he said hoarsely. "Everything you touch turns to slime! But not her!" He shifted his gaze to Raven, and his tone pleaded with the rough, rusty sound of a man who never had to plead for anything. "Raven, don't let him do this to you. It's not too late to get away from him!"

She looked at him in faint amusement, the perfect image of a woman who seduced—but was never seduced herself. "Don't be ridiculous, Josh," she said gently.

Josh made a wrenching attempt to free himself, ignoring the urgent mutters of Rafferty and Lucas. "Raven . . ." It was almost a groan. "Please! He'll turn you into something ugly, something vile—"

"I told you in New York, Josh." She was still gentle. "I told you not to follow me. I'd rather be my own woman than just an ornament on any man's arm."

"Dammit, you know I don't—I want to *marry* you!"

Her eyes went suddenly cold and hard, and her voice was filled with scorn. "You want to *own* me, the way you own hotels and corporations and the two men trying to keep you from making a fool of yourself!"

"Raven!"

"Get him out of here," she advised his men coolly, expressionless again. "And try to keep him out of my sight from now on."

"Josh, come on!" Rafferty and Lucas struggled against the distraught man's nearly overpowering strength, and finally managed to hustle their friend out the door.

"Raven!" The final cry was despairing, defeated. A magnificent performance.

From behind his column, Theodore said blankly, "Well, for God's sake!"

Smoothly, as if nothing had happened, Leon said merely, "Tomorrow, Theodore," and escorted Raven out through the front doors and to his limo.

Once they were in the car and on their way to a restaurant, he murmured, "Joshua Long. He seems obsessed with you, my dear. Does he know—?"

Raven uttered a low laugh that would have shamed uncaring ice. "Do you imagine he'd become involved with any woman without checking into her background? Certainly he knows what I—do for a living. I believe the poor man's appalled at himself. But he's too accustomed to molding his empire; he wishes to reform me, if you please. Obviously, he believes you to be a bad influence on me. The fool."

"Ah." From the dimness of the limo, Travers said somewhat dryly, "They say that many a bad woman has been a good man's downfall."

A gambler by nature, Raven took a chance and retorted indifferently, "I believe the opposite is more commonly true."

"Very likely, my dear." His voice was indifferent as well. "Very likely. Shall we return to that Italian place you enjoyed so much?"

• • •

"Whew!" Rafferty shook his numbed hand and sent a reproachful look at Josh. "Did you *have* to twist like that? I think my wrist is sprained."

They were sitting in a darkened car near Travers's apartment building, and even though Josh was still too worried to feel humorous, he grinned faintly as he lit a cigarette. "Sorry about that. Had to make it look good."

"We know," Lucas remarked from the backseat. "But you don't know your own strength. Hagen should have sent Zach after all."

"And speaking of our security chief," Rafferty said, "shouldn't we be getting back to ease his worried mind? We've rung down the curtain on our little drama."

Bracing himself for their reaction, Josh said, "You two go on back. I'm staying."

"What?" Rafferty's voice was faint.

The red glow of Josh's cigarette brightened as he drew on it strongly. "I said I'm staying. I'm going in the back entrance, and I'll be in the penthouse when Raven gets home."

Lucas leaned forward to peer into the front seat. "Josh, you know Hagen told us none too politely to keep our paws out of this from now on."

Politely, Josh offered a rude message for Hagen in basic Anglo-Saxon language.

"No," Lucas said with a sigh, leaning back. "I won't tell him that. Fire me, if you like."

"Me too," Rafferty chimed in.

The moment Raven entered the penthouse, she knew Josh was there. It was not her training or experience that told her of his presence, or even her exceptionally alert senses. She simply knew. Quickly, she dropped her purse on the table beside the silk flowers and turned on the tape player. And she had taken no more than half a dozen steps across the deep white carpet, when he came silently out of her bedroom.

"You took a chance," she said. "Leon might have come in with me."

"That's why I was in the bedroom." He glanced toward the player, then lifted a questioning brow.

"There's a bug in those flowers," she explained, trying to keep her voice steady. "The player jams it."

"Any more bugs in here?" He was moving toward her, unable to keep his eyes off the stunning picture she made in a lime green silk sheath that glimmered in the faint lamplight and made her eyes a mysterious shade that was nearly green.

He had almost forgotten his role hours earlier because of how lovely she looked.

"No." She cleared her throat, discovering that it didn't help the huskiness of her voice. "I check every day."

"I was careful," he told her, halting an arm's length away to gaze down at her. "I know more than I want to about covert operations and the like; I didn't make a sound until you came in. But I couldn't stay away." He took her hand, looking down at the slim, ringless fingers, then led her to the couch and pulled her gently down beside him. "Did Travers buy it?"

"Yes, I'm almost sure he did."

"Almost," Josh noted bleakly. "You can never be sure of anything in your work, can you?"

"I'm sure of myself." Her voice was steady, though

still husky. "I have to be. I spend so much time building an image of myself for other people to believe that I'd get lost if I weren't sure of who I really am."

Josh leaned back, still holding her hand, looking at her. "Tell me about Raven," he murmured. "Tell me about the life that shaped such a remarkable woman."

Raven looked down at their clasped hands for a moment, watching his thumb brush over hers again and again, almost a compulsive movement, and she was very conscious of the intimacy between them. The quiet apartment. The darkness of night outside. The feeling that they had locked out danger for a while. Returning her gaze to his, she had to swallow suddenly, because she had never seen such a look in a man's eyes before.

"It's . . . an ordinary life, most of it," she answered at last. "I'm a service brat; Pop was career army, stationed all over the world. I had an aptitude for languages—or maybe it was just exposure. I picked up half a dozen languages by the time I was sixteen. Tara was my older sister. We were close."

His hand tightened on hers, and Raven shook off the dark thoughts. She managed a laugh. "My name isn't Anderson, by the way. It's O'Malley. I stick with my first name as often as I can; it makes things simpler."

Josh, even though he was conscious of the danger surrounding her and aware of the urge to grab what he could because there very well might be no tomorrow for them, kept an iron rein on the demands of his desire. He had seen shadows in her eyes whenever she remembered her sister, but he didn't have to be told this lovely woman had seen too much these last years to have escaped being scarred by other things.

Thinking of that, he said quietly, "You've given up a great deal for your work. A personal life. Even a secure identity. Friends who know who you are. A home. Or is there a home you go back to?"

She shook her head. "Not really. My parents live in Seattle, but they don't know what I'm doing; I didn't want to worry them. I had an apartment at first, but it hardly seemed worth the bother. I was rarely in it. Hagen's team is a small one, so we're all—well, utilized pretty frequently. I'm out of the country more often than in."

"The other apartment," Josh said slowly. "Does it really belong to friends?"

Her smile was brief, mirthless. "No. The manager thinks so, of course; I had all the proper authorization. The tenants went through a reputable agency to sublet; they have no idea that their apartment is being used as a safe house. But I need that. I need a secure place to unwind."

Josh was very still. His own life had been unusual, his childhood made hideous by his mother's death and the cloak-and-dagger threats of Stuart's top secret work. And even though he'd grown up largely away from that, the wealth he'd inherited at an early age had made him something apart from other children and, later, other men. Even though he knew close friendship with the three men who were far more than employees, he also knew the loneliness of being different.

And Raven's unconsciously stark words told him as nothing else could that she, too, was different from other women. For years she had balanced dangerously between two worlds, snatching a moment here and there for a breath drawn without tension. Assuming roles with an expertise any Hollywood actress would have envied, and maintaining those deadly roles in the face of unspeakable pressures. She might be a woman who had learned ruthless methods of protecting and defending herself, yet she could still smile at a man with laughter in her eyes.

Josh shook his head half-consciously, unable to tear his gaze away from those incredible violet eyes. She could have had the world, he thought dimly, could have accomplished anything she had wanted, reached any pinnacle. But she had turned her back on personal goals, choosing to walk the dark side of the street and use her talents in fighting back that darkness.

"You make me feel ashamed," he said huskily. "Everything that I have . . . and I've done so little. When I'm asked to help, I do. But I wait to be asked. You never have."

Raven was shaken. "Josh, so many people depend on you. So many have good jobs and earn good money because you care enough to be fair." Her laugh was unsteady. "I've seen *your* file, remember? Endowments for hospitals and universities, support for orphanages, endless programs designed by you and your companies to help people. You think that doesn't matter? Well, it does. It matters a helluva lot. You do *so much*! Your companies devoted over half their profits last year to helping people."

Josh found a small, wry smile. "Even a playboy can have a conscience."

She chuckled. "I didn't mean that, and you know

it! I was mad, that's all. And more than a little shocked to find out you really *were* a prince."

"No. No prince. Just a man, Raven." He sighed raggedly, his hand tightening around hers. "I haven't walked on the dark side like you, but I've seen it. And it scares the hell out of me to think of you being there."

"Josh—"

He reached for her, caught in the overpowering hunger to hold her in his arms, to feel her against him. But she pulled back abruptly, and he froze, searching her eyes. "If you want me to leave—" He could barely get the words out, his heart pounding sickly in his chest.

She lifted her free hand to touch his cheek, her eyes very dark and a curiously shy smile on her face. "No. But whenever I've been with Leon, I feel . . . Do you mind if I take a shower? I want to wash away Leon and that person I am when I'm with him."

Josh held her hand to his cheek, turning briefly to press a kiss into her palm. "Go ahead," he said gently. "But remember something, Raven. He could never make you dirty. No one could ever make you dirty."

Too restless to be still after she'd gone into the bedroom, Josh rose and began pacing slowly. The heavy drapes were drawn, but he stayed away from the windows, knowing that if there were any watching eyes, it would be dangerous to show them a male silhouette while Raven was supposed to be alone.

He paced and tried not to think of her in the shower; she needed this time alone, he knew, and he was determined to do nothing to disturb her.

But *he* was disturbed. He had no doubt at all about his own feelings, but Raven, though wonderfully responsive physically, had said nothing about her own feelings for him. He told himself it was unfair of him to expect her to love him as instantly and completely as he loved her. She was, heaven knew, occupied by other and far more dangerous matters and had been since before they'd met.

That knowledge didn't lessen his fear. She had appeared suddenly out of her shadowy life, and he knew only too well that she could choose to return there. And with all his resources, all the wealth and power at his command, Josh knew, too, that if she vanished by choice, he would never be able to find her.

He stood motionless in the center of the room, staring blindly at the wall, nothing but bleak images filling his mind. She had the ability to love, he knew, but would she make that choice? With everything she had seen and done these last years, what man could hope to keep her at his side unless she chose to be there? It would be like trying to cage the wind.

Even through his dark thoughts, Josh heard the distant sound of the shower stop, and he listened for a few moments until he heard a hair dryer begin to buzz. *Even her hair*, he thought somberly. *Even her hair feels dirty to her when she's left him.*

And there was that. Raven knew herself, but Josh believed she had scars deep inside from the cruel cuts of the roles she had to play. It was impossible to walk on the dark side without garnering scars. And Raven felt dirty. What had that done to her feelings of self-worth, to her femininity? What kind of strength would it demand from a woman to rise above the shadowy corridors of a separate and ugly life?

Abruptly, Josh shrugged out of his jacket and threw it across the couch, moving swiftly and silently toward the bedroom. He went into the softly lighted room, barely glancing at the ultra-feminine decor. She was sitting at the dressing table in the white silk robe she'd worn earlier, a brush in one hand and the dryer in the other. Her steady, rhythmic motions with the brush stopped as she caught sight of him in the mirror, but she said nothing.

Halting behind her, Josh took the brush and dryer from her hands and began using them. He was awkward at first, but his movements became rhythmic and sure before long. The heavy mass of her wet hair lightened as it dried, and deep, warm highlights glowed in the dark brunette tresses. Each stroke of the brush caused her hair to shimmer more, the silky touch of it against his hand a feather-light caress.

Absorbed in his task, Josh watched her hair become a vital, living mass of darkness. He looked up once to meet her eyes in the mirror and his hand faltered. Her gaze was fixed on his face, eyelids heavy; her lips were parted softly and the white silk covering her breasts rose and fell quickly.

Josh swallowed, his jaw tensing as he pulled his gaze from hers and concentrated on what he was doing. His fingers were white-knuckled around the handle of the dryer, but even then he couldn't hold it steady. His chest hurt and every muscle in his body felt rigid, while the deep, slow pulse of desire given life by their first meeting grew stronger and tauter.

He had more or less earned the outdated sobriquet of playboy, Josh knew. His sister Serena had often scoffed at his efforts to keep control of his life by subsisting on "a steady diet of blondes." And Josh was a sensual man; he had found pleasure with those blondes. But he had never before felt this vital need, this pulsing of his entire body in an ache for one woman—and only one woman.

He turned off the dryer and set the brush aside, moving slowly, his eyes again fixed on hers. She turned on the low stool and rose to face him, and Josh knew there was no scrap of lace and silk beneath the robe this time.

His hand lifted to touch her cheek, the herbal scent of the soap she'd used making him dizzy again. Or maybe it wasn't the soap. "When you came home," he said hoarsely, "I didn't dare kiss you. I knew I wouldn't be able to stop."

Her slender hands rose to lie against his chest, and then her fingers began slowly unfastening the buttons of his shirt. Her eyes were dark, as enigmatic as those of a cat. "No interruptions tonight," she whispered. "Let the world stop for a while. Let it all stop for a while."

If there was desperation in her words, it was muted and neither of them really heard it.

Josh shrugged out of his shirt, biting back a groan when he felt her hands slide down over his chest and stomach until his belt buckle stopped the contact of flesh on flesh. His own hands felt the cool touch of silk when he reached for her, drawing her abruptly against him, and his mouth found her parted lips hungrily.

Raven slid her hands along his ribs and then up his back, vaguely conscious of his hands holding her, one tangled in her hair and the other at her hips. She could feel his hard body burning her, imprinting itself on hers, and she rose on tiptoe until she fit him perfectly. Only the scant barrier of silk separated them, and she felt her breasts swell and begin to throb even as another ache grew deep inside her.

He possessed her mouth as if only that kept him from dying, as if he were starved and the touch of her sated hunger. His tongue sought the tender sweetness of her mouth and Raven responded instantly, exploring as he did, caressing in the secret, hidden kiss of lovers. She felt her robe slide to the floor and her soft whimper was lost in his mouth as the sensual rasp of his hair-covered chest turned her nipples to fire.

The room seemed to move around them, and Raven half-opened her eyes as his mouth reluctantly left hers. She realized that he had picked her up effortlessly and was carrying her to the bed. Raven wasn't a small woman, and the ease with which he carried her was a faint, almost instinctive shock. It disturbed her, but nothing could put out the fire he had ignited in her body.

Josh managed to strip the covers back toward the foot of the bed before lowering her onto its softness, then straightened and rapidly discarded his remaining clothing. His eyes, wild and glittering, raked her body with an intensity Raven could feel in every nerve, and she could barely stop looking at his face long enough to absorb the powerful strength of his body as it was revealed to her.

Her breath caught in her throat and Raven knew a single fleeting moment of panic, instantly overborne by an equally strong wave of primitive desire. Clothed, he was an impressive figure, tall and broad-shouldered, with an easy, athletic grace of movement. But when the trappings of civilization fell away, he was something else, something elementary. Raw sexuality emanated from his muscled body like a primitive aura, and his desire was a vital, living force she could feel, as if electricity had been loosed in the room.

The strength of her own response to his power frightened her, and that instinctive fear quivered in her voice. "Josh . . ."

"Shhh." He was with her, kissing her slowly, deeply, raised on an elbow beside her with one hand lying quietly over the sensitive flesh of her stomach. "You're so beautiful," he murmured, his lips feathering over her face, and his voice was unsteady. "I love you, Raven."

She found his shoulders and held on, needing . . . needing. Fear ebbed, and all her senses focused on his lips, on the hand still lying unmoving just beneath her breasts. Tension began winding tightly within her, as much emotional as physical, and she could feel something else inside, something still and dark. And Josh felt it as well.

He lifted his head briefly, those hot, glittering eyes looking deeply into her own, and the rough sound he made was one of pain. "Don't . . . don't hold back, darling. Don't hide from me."

Was she hiding? Raven didn't know. But she

had never in her life given herself up totally just to feeling, and the guards that necessity had helped her build around her emotions and her mind weren't easily released. She *wanted* to lose herself in Josh, in the way he made her feel, but years of tense, careful living had left their mark.

"I . . ." She tried to catch her breath, tried to combat the smothering feeling weighing her down. "I don't want to . . . I can't help it, Josh. . . ."

For an instant he was still, tense, and then his head lowered again and his mouth found hers with a gentleness all the more astonishing because she could feel the rigid muscles of his body demanding more, much more than a kiss. But he was careful, inexpressibly tender, as if there were no hurry. His tongue traced the sensitive inner surface of her lips softly; his teeth caught her lower lip gently; he brushed his mouth against hers lightly again and again.

The careful, insidiously seductive caresses dissolved Raven's defenses as no demand ever could. The dark stillness within her faded away and tension grew. But this tension was sweet, shattering, and seemed to be centered deep within her. She felt his hand finally move, tracing the lower curves of her breasts, sweeping lightly down over her stomach and back again.

Raven looked at him when he lifted his head, staring at his absorbed face, quivering as his hand gently molded her breasts to fit his palm. He seemed mesmerized by her response to his touch; his gaze was fixed on her breasts and her nipples hardened achingly even as he merely looked at them. Then his mouth touched the slope of her breast, trailing toward the yearning point with agonizing slowness.

All fears and barriers forgotten, Raven thought of nothing but her body's need for him. And when his mouth at last closed hotly on her nipple, she moaned at the instant wave of burning pleasure that swept her entire body. Her fingers locked in his hair and she tried to hold herself still for that nerve-shattering caress, even though her body needed desperately to move.

She could feel his hand moving down her hip, then skim tantalizingly up the inside of one thigh, and the hollowness within her seemed to swell achingly. She was raw nerves and empty need, and the combination nearly drove her mad. She couldn't breathe, her heart was pounding out of control, and his hand was stroking the inner thighs parting mindlessly for his touch.

Raven gasped, her body arching in a sudden, helpless reaction when his fingers found the warm, vulnerable flesh they sought. His mouth moved from one breast to the other, tongue swirling maddeningly, while his fingers stroked gently, insistently.

"Josh!"

"Shhh." He didn't trust his own voice and could only draw a harsh breath when his head lifted. He couldn't take his eyes off her tense, striving face, watching her faint, jerky movements as awakened senses took control of her body. His own body was hard and throbbing, and he thought he'd explode, but he was drunk on the touch of her, the taste of her.

He had managed to rein his desperate need because of the far more imperative need to reassure her, to ease his way past the barriers he'd felt in her mind and, perhaps, her soul. And now he held on to those restraints fiercely, all his consciousness bent on pleasing her.

He flicked a pointed nipple with his tongue again and again, then captured it hungrily. The kittenlike sounds she made drove him crazy, and his hand moved more insistently. Then he felt her explode, and she cried out softly as her body convulsed.

Blind and deaf to everything but the shattering waves of sensation racing through her body, Raven clung to him, shaking, the world revolving behind her closed eyelids. Nothing in her life had prepared her for this wild, mind-numbing pleasure, and she lost herself in the rippling waves of it.

Josh, his own need critical, gave her no time to examine these strange new feelings. His hands caressed her shaking body with undiminished hunger, and his lips trailed fire everywhere they touched.

Dazed, she stared up at his hard, intent face, and the molten heat in the pit of her belly renewed itself in an astonishing explosion that seared her nerve endings. Her desire was so intense, it was as if it were new again, surging powerfully within her, but this time she was all the more conscious of the emptiness. Where there had been shivering pleasure before was only a yearning, throbbing ache, and she knew she'd go mad if he didn't ease that ache, fill that emptiness.

Instinctively trying to draw him closer, Raven almost sobbed with relief when he moved between her thighs and braced himself above her. His chest moved strongly with each ragged breath, and every muscle of his body was tense with strain, but still he hesitated, gazing down at her with hot eyes.

"I love you," he said raspingly, his voice all but gone. "I've always loved you. . . ."

Raven felt a pressure against her aching flesh, and she barely caught her breath before a sharp pain tore a faint cry from her throat. Even as she saw Josh's eyes darken in a quick reaction, she felt her body stretching, accepting him, and her own eyes widened at the primitive sensation.

His body shuddered, but Josh was still, gazing down at her with something she'd never seen before in his eyes, something very like wonder. "Raven . . ." he whispered.

She surged upward then, taking all of him, and her own whisper was fierce and sure. "I love you." Her arms pulled him closer and she gloried in the hot, slick union of their bodies. "Josh . . ."

A wild tangle of emotions nearly ended Josh's control, but he hung on and began moving with all the care his strained body could manage. He had wanted her willing and wild beneath him, and now that he had it, he wanted to make it last forever.

One silken thigh brushed his hip in a nerve-shattering caress, and Josh groaned, his measured movements quickening in the instinctive drive toward release, and the coiling tension within him wound so tightly it was a quivering ache.

Her fingers dug into his shoulders and those glorious long legs cradled him passionately; when she whimpered softly, he lost control. His body buried itself in her again and again, striving to have more of her, all of her.

He was wilder than he'd meant to be, but her

soft little cries were driving him crazy and her body sheathed his with a caressing tightness that made savage ripples of pleasure race through him. And she was moving with him, as fierce and driven as he, as desperate.

Then she surged against him wildly, crying out, and her hot flare of pleasure caught him in its force. He buried himself in her with a hoarse sound, shuddering violently as waves of ecstasy jolted through him in a release so devastatingly complete he thought he had died. . . .

Six

A cool breeze from the air-conditioning system played over their damp, entwined bodies, and Josh managed to pull the covers up over them without losing his possessive hold on Raven. The lamplit room was quiet now, and his voice was hushed when he spoke. "Why didn't you tell me?"

"Maybe I thought you wouldn't believe me." She cuddled closer to his side, her body limp and her mind floating peacefully.

Josh was stroking her long hair, his hand still a bit unsteady. "Did you think that?"

She was quiet a moment, then sighed. "No. I can't imagine another man who would have believed me, but I know you would have. Some women in this business . . . well, sex is a tool to them, to use like a smile or a certain dress or a gun. I was just never willing to use it. And until I met you—"

Josh raised himself on an elbow and gazed down at her with darkened, tender eyes. "I'm glad," he said simply. "It wouldn't have changed anything, but I'm glad."

She smiled. "So am I."

He traced the slightly swollen curve of her lower lip, still unable to stop gazing at her. "I thought I heard you tell me something else, though," he murmured.

Her response was unhesitating. "I love you, Josh."

With an odd, rough little sound, he lowered his head to kiss her very gently. "I was afraid to hope for that. You came into my life so suddenly, I was afraid you'd leave it the same way." Then he stilled. "You won't, will you?"

This time, she hesitated. "Josh, I've never thought much about tomorrow, even when I could. Before. And these last years . . . well, I've seen things I'll never forget as long as I live. Ugly things. You said it yourself. I've walked on the dark side for a long time."

Josh was afraid he looked grim. He felt grim. But his voice was very soft. "Do you mean you don't want to stop your work? Or that you're afraid that work has changed you in some way that would make leaving it behind you impossible?"

She answered slowly, carefully choosing her words. "This kind of work isn't something you plan to make a career of; it's too easy to burn out, lose effectiveness. I don't want to stop helping, Josh, but I want to stop working the way I have been."

He nodded, expecting nothing else from her. "And the second question? Are you afraid you won't be able to leave it behind you?"

"I just don't know." Raven felt the sense of

wellbeing slipping from her grasp, and a little voice inside her warned that it would always be that way. She tried to speak lightly, tried, as always, to fight back shadows with a laugh. "I've never fallen in love before; give me time to figure things out."

Josh's expression was still serious, and a muscle briefly worked in his jaw. But his kiss was gentle. "I've been rushing you since the night we met, haven't I?"

"Oh, you noticed that?"

He kissed her again, not quite as gently this time, and both felt the inexorable rise of desire. A bit thickly, Josh asked, "Am I rushing you now?"

Raven wound her arms around his neck, losing herself in sensation as his mouth found her breast. "Who cares?" she murmured, and forgot the world again.

Rafferty looked up from the papers spread out on the desk and peered at Zach as the big man moved restlessly to the bar and fixed himself a drink. "Go to bed," the lawyer advised dryly.

"I don't see you sleeping."

"That's because your summons caught me in the middle of a case; I have to work sometime, don't I?" He wasn't really surprised that Zach barely listened.

Zach stared at his empty glass as if it had offended him in some way. "Dammit, he should be back by now. He should have been back hours ago. It's three o'clock."

"He won't be back before dawn," Rafferty said calmly. "If then."

"It's dangerous."

"Of course it's dangerous." ⸗

Zach sat down on the couch and pulled a deck of cards toward him, then began to deal a hand of solitaire. "Dammit," he grunted morosely.

Lucas emerged from his bedroom in a robe, but looked alert. "You two would wake the dead," he complained in the tone of a man who just wanted something to say and didn't particularly care what it was.

Rafferty, a little amused, sat back in his chair and sighed. "Look, guys, he's a big boy."

"Who?" Lucas asked rather unconvincingly.

Zach placed a black nine on a black ten, and frowned at the result. "You two shouldn't have let him go in there alone," he said.

"I didn't think he needed any help," Rafferty said.

Lucas poured a drink for himself and then promptly ignored it to pace over to the window. "Be daylight in a couple of hours," he said to no one in particular.

Gathering up his papers, Rafferty said in a brisk tone, "He'll fire all three of us if he finds us waiting up for him."

Lucas swung around to face them. "Maybe we should—"

"No," the lawyer said instantly.

Zach sighed and agreed heavily, casting his cards aside. "No. He sure wouldn't thank us for it. In fact, he'd probably fire all three of us. He'd be with her right now even if she were on the deck of the *Titanic*."

"Or inside the gates of hell," Rafferty acknowledged softly. "It must be something to feel like that. It must really be something."

There was a smothering sensation of dread and the sick feeling of being surrounded by icy shadows and menacing movements more felt than seen. The same nightmare, always the same, and she knew that the shadows would go away if she could only wake herself up and turn on a light. But she'd see Tara's face, Tara's body, if she turned on the light; that was what kept her trapped in the darkness. She couldn't bear to see Tara again, not like that, not the way she had been in that awful house. It would happen all over again. She'd blindly feel her way through that dark smoky room and turn on a light, only to see her sister . . . the dying creature her sister had become. Darkness was closing around her and she moaned, cold and alone, unable to turn on a light and leave the darkness that was choking her.

Then she heard a low sound, gentle and soothing, and felt sudden warmth wrap around her. The darkness receded slowly and she could breathe again.

For the first time, she didn't wake screaming.

Josh, still shaken, held her close to him, his hands stroking her hair soothingly. The sound she had made in her sleep had been a soft one, but it had chased chills through him. The sound of an animal in pain. He lifted a hand to stroke her cheek and forehead, relieved to find the clamminess gone.

The lamp was still on, and he stared at the ceiling while she slept in apparent peace beside him. Nightmares. Shadows from the past? He could guess the cause, and wondered if Raven would be haunted always by the sister she had found dying.

Was that the part of her past that forever would color the present and future? Or could he somehow reach into a guarded, wounded soul and help heal her? Josh didn't know.

He knew only that he had to. Somehow.

Josh woke in the faint gray of dawn, instantly aware of coldness, where before there had been warmth. He half-sat up in a quick movement, then stilled as he saw her by the window. She was wearing the white robe and stood well to one side of the window, where no one watching from outside could have seen her, barely lifting the heavy drape to look out.

Her expression was intense; Josh didn't think she was conscious at all of her guardedness. And that somehow made it all the more chilling.

"Raven?"

She turned, smiling, and moved toward the bed. "Good morning." She drew one leg up as she sat on the bed, the short robe parting to bare her thigh, and Josh found his hand going to her silken flesh as though drawn by a magnet.

"Good morning." He curled his free hand around her neck, drawing her gently forward for his kiss, and then sent a very reluctant glance toward the light struggling to penetrate the drapes. "I suppose I should leave."

"Probably." Her smile wavered for an instant. "If you were seen leaving, it could be dangerous for you. But—"

"But?"

"I don't want you to go."

He kissed her again, gazing into her eyes. "Do you have to see him today?"

Raven didn't need the question clarified. "This afternoon—and tonight."

"Then I can stay for a while."

She hesitated. "Training and experience tell me you shouldn't. It would be taking a chance, a big chance. What Hagen would call an unnecessary risk. But I've given Leon and the security people the impression that I stay up late and sleep late; no one ever disturbs me until afternoon."

Josh just barely could hear the music from her "jamming" tape player in the living room, and nodded in that direction. "Won't anyone wonder about that? It's been playing all night."

Raven shook her head. "No, I often play it all night. On the theory that if you let people get used to something, they don't pay any attention at all to it after a while."

He brushed the dark, heavy hair away from her face and looked at her steadily, the love he felt very nearly overwhelming him. "I don't want to do anything to put you or me in greater danger, but I don't want to leave you."

She didn't hesitate this time. "Stay."

They couldn't completely shut out the world, but they did manage to forget it. For a while. The warm, wet intimacy of a shared shower sent them back to bed, and the sun was well up when they made it to the kitchen for a breakfast of sorts. Neither dressed, because each glance caught and held, and getting rid of clothing was a waste of precious time.

Josh was conscious of that passing time, aware of the uncertain footing beneath them. Reluctant to press her for a commitment, he fought the instincts urging him to grab her and hold on tight. It was a next to impossible task, because Raven was so instantly and utterly responsive . . . yet her eyes remained enigmatic.

He was not a man who had felt uncertain of himself ever before in his life, but during that morning he learned the terrors of uncertainty. She had said that she loved him, and Josh believed her. She loved him, and yet their future was very much in doubt in spite of it. And not only because of her background but his own, he realized.

"Does who I am bother you?" he asked late that morning. Reluctantly, he was dressing to go, and Raven was curled up in the bed watching him.

She blinked, then smiled. "I'm not sure. It scares me a little, I think."

Josh sat down on the edge of the bed and frowned. "Why?"

"Because you're so visible." She spoke slowly, obviously searching herself. "And I've never been visible. That file on you is incredible; everything you do is news. You and the people you know are world movers."

"I'm just a man, Raven. Don't ever forget that. And I don't plan to be so visible in the future. I've had that. I have four houses—but none of them is *home*. I want a real home now. With you." His hand reached out and lay warmly over the sheet covering her flat stomach. "Children."

"I can't think past today," she whispered, trying not to imagine what it woud be like to carry their child, trying not to let the magic of such a vision seduce her.

After a moment, Josh nodded. He leaned down to kiss her gently, but with an edge of desperation he wasn't able to hide. And he could barely get out the words that were more plea than command: "Just promise me—"

"I won't leave." Her voice was steady. "I won't run away from this." She pushed a lock of black hair off his forehead.

He couldn't ask for more, no matter how much he wanted to.

Raven was to meet Leon at his office building, and her alter ego was firmly in place when she ordered a security man at the door to park her Mercedes in the underground garage. She was cool and composed as she went up in the elevator. Still, despite her training and experience, the fact that her life had been changed the night before had left its mark.

For five years, she had lived in a world where there was, as Josh had observed, nothing certain. Every stranger met was a potential enemy, and it had been only rare moments, such as her meeting with him, when she had ignored the danger and suspicions that shadowed her life. She had all but forgotten how to open up to another human being, share herself.

But last night had changed her. Like a steeple-chase jockey who made plans only "after the last race," she couldn't look ahead until danger was past. Was that sheer superstition or just her innate realism?

But she loved Josh, loved him with a depth and certainty she hadn't thought possible, and in a soft and secure corner of her mind she allowed herself to dream.

On the surface, however, Raven Anderson was the ice maiden, and it was this woman who lifted a cool brow at Theodore when she found him alone in Leon's office.

"Miss Howard wasn't at her desk," she said, referring to Leon's excellent secretary. "Where's Leon?"

Spaniel eyes blinked behind his thick glasses as Theodore came forward to meet her with a blend of anxiety and entreaty. "They needed him downstairs, Miss Anderson; he asked me to make sure you were comfortable until he returned."

Indifferently, she said, "I'll be fine, Theodore. You needn't wait."

He came a step closer and licked his lips nervously. "You're a beautiful woman, Miss, er, Raven."

"Thank you." Her voice was cold now, and she fought the urge to back away when he came closer still. She didn't like the man; his anxious mannerisms made her somehow nervous, and the memory of his cold hands touching her once before had stayed with her a long time.

"I could fix you a drink," he offered, his eyes focusing on her breasts.

"No."

He glanced toward the closed door. "Leon'll be a while. Why don't we get comfortable on the couch?"

"You could learn a lot from Leon, Theodore."

She stared coldly at him, her distaste obvious. "He never makes clumsy passes."

Theodore's pale face flushed. "Don't be so high and mighty," he said, his voice abruptly derisive. "I know what you are, *Miss Anderson.* You're worse than a whore. You buy and sell decent girls and make them into whores."

Deep inside her in a cold place, Raven marked yet another score to be settled with him. But her voice remained coolly indifferent, and her expression was faintly amused. "The pot sneering at the kettle, don't you think? You work for Leon, and that makes you a pimp."

Theodore caught her suddenly around her waist. His face was more deeply flushed and his eyes held an avid expression. "Pimps try out their girls," he said hoarsely. But a ringing slap sent him staggering back with a curse and one hand held to his cheek.

"I think not. I'm not one of your girls. I also don't belong to Leon, luckily for you. Get out of here."

"You'll regret that!" he said shakily.

Bored, Raven turned toward the bar and fixed herself a drink. She didn't change expression even when the door slammed behind Theodore. Wandering to the window with her glass, she stood gazing out. Still performing. But this time, it was for the eye of a hidden camera. It was there, she knew, recording everyone who visited Leon's office.

A few moments later he came in, and she had to wonder coldly if she had just passed another test. Impossible to tell, of course, from Leon's bland, smiling face.

"Good afternoon, my dear. Sorry to keep you waiting."

"No problem." She watched him put away some papers in his desk, just barely catching the slight flick of his fingers on the underside of the desk. Her mind worked instantly, rapidly. Had he turned off a hidden tape recorder? The camera?

In a gentle tone, Leon said, "Unwise, my dear, to provoke Theodore."

Unmoved, she said, "Did you expect me to tumble onto the couch for him, Leon? Was I supposed to do so because he works for you and you expect me to keep the help happy?"

"Did I ask you to?"

"You tell me."

As always his gray eyes were unreadable. "No, my dear, I did not ask you. But Theodore is an unstable personality. Surely you've noticed? And you're a survivor. It might perhaps have been wiser if you had . . . sunk your scruples?"

"Not that far." She turned away from the window to place her empty glass on the bar. Boldly, she forced the issue. "Enjoyable as your company is, Leon, I came here to fulfill a commission. Not to be pawed by a rabbity office boy. My clients are becoming impatient."

"You spoke to them?"

Raven didn't fall into the trap. "No. But I have a deadline, and I know my clients."

Leon's fingers flickered again beneath the desk, and that bothered Raven, for some reason. Especially when he continued on the subject she had opened.

"I believe you are well-versed in your clients' . . . tastes?"

"I know what they want."

"Excellent. It will take a day or so to make the arrangements."

"No blind sales, Leon." She looked at him coolly. "I expect to examine the merchandise."

"Of course." He locked his desk, then came forward to lead her toward the door. "I will arrange it. And, by the way, my dear, I've never called you a whore. Never again call me a pimp."

Raven's mask held—just. There had been a steely warning in his gentle tone. "My apologies, Leon," she said.

Josh lit a cigarette and spoke into the phone. "And then?"

"And then they went to a restaurant," Lucas reported briefly. "Just the two of them, boss. I can see both entrances from here; they're still inside."

"All right. Let me know when they start back to the penthouse."

Lucas hesitated. "Boss . . . they'll never know they're being followed, but do you think this is smart? We were told to lay off."

"I don't trust Hagen's so-called security measures," Josh said flatly. "She's in danger every moment she's with Travers, and I want them watched."

"You sign the checks." Lucas sighed. "And I haven't seen a sign of surveillance other than mine."

"That's good enough for me."

Doubtful, Lucas said, "Well, hell, Josh, these

guys are supposed to be pros; they could be all around me and I'd never see them."

"You'd see them." In spite of worry, Josh smiled a little. "Is this the ex-cop the feds have been trying to entice away from me for years? The cop who was undercover for ten months to break a drug ring?"

"Bygone days," Lucas said. "I'm getting old and rusty."

"You're a year younger than I am," Josh retorted mildly.

"Well, *you* looked a mite weary this afternoon."

"Never mind."

Laughing, Lucas said, "I'll check in when anything changes." He hung up.

Rafferty shoved a paper across the desk to Josh. "Sign this."

Obediently, Josh signed.

Glancing over at Zach, who was seated nearby, Rafferty said, "I could steal him blind; he never reads *anything*."

"You read it, didn't you?" Josh asked absently.

Sighing, Rafferty filed the signed paper in his briefcase. "Uh-huh."

Josh smiled suddenly. "Why do you think I pay you such an exorbitant salary? So I won't have to read. What *was* that, anyway?"

"You just gave away money," Rafferty told him politely.

"To who? Whom."

"Serena's latest orphanage."

Josh eyed his attorney thoughtfully. "If I remember correctly, you said the last time she wanted an endowment fund set up that you were proof against Rena's wiles."

Rafferty examined his fingernails. "Yes. Well." Looking up to meet amused eyes, he said accusingly, "Even if I managed *not* to succumb, you would. I just thought I'd save time and draw up the damned papers."

Zach, who had let most of the conversation pass unheard, looked up then from the computer print-out he was studying. "Did you know Travers had a wife?"

Josh looked over at his security chief. "Had. She died years ago, didn't she?"

"Yeah." Zach frowned. "Three years ago. His yacht went down, and they never found her body. Says here, he was in Geneva at the time. Police put the blame on a boiler explosion."

"It happens," Rafferty noted. "Not that I'd know about yachts, of course. My clutch-fisted employer—"

"Is going to dock your salary for that remark," Josh told him. Then he sighed and his mind, never far from thoughts of Raven, returned completely to her. There was so much in this situation he couldn't hope to control, and the danger she faced scared him half to death. "I hope to high heaven she's all right."

"She is," the lawyer told him firmly. "Lucas is on watch, and you know he's damned good."

Josh stubbed out his cigarette and immediately lit another, and tried to feel reassured by Rafferty's remark. "I know. It's just— Dammit, everything could blow up in her face; Travers is about as stable as nitro." He frowned a few moments in brooding silence. "Zach? Get me a gun, will you?"

The big security chief looked up, his abstracted expression instantly replaced by faint anxiety. "Josh—"

"Is that a problem?"

"No. But—"

"I promise not to shoot my foot off, all right?"

Zach knew there was little danger of that, since Josh was expert with firearms, and the impatience in Josh's voice was obvious; he didn't intend to argue about this. Sighing, he murmured, "I'll have it by tomorrow."

"Thank you."

"I'm not worried about job security," Rafferty said as if to a fourth party. "Even if Josh gets his head blown off, I happen to know that Serena is currently his heir. She'll keep us all busy for years."

"That reminds me—" Josh was frowning.

"Yes," Rafferty murmured. "I thought it would."

Fretfully, Kelsey said, "He's following them—that detective of Long's."

"Of course," Hagen said calmly.

The redhead shot a quick glance at his boss. "You warned them, didn't you?"

"Certainly."

"But you aren't surprised?"

Hagen lit a fat cigar and contemplated it with an air of satisfaction. "My boy, when you've studied human nature as long as I have, you'll discover that people are rarely surprising."

Kelsey concentrated on staying well back from Lucas Kendrick's rented car, frowning. "Amateurs. They're going to botch it," he said gloomily.

In a conversational tone, Hagen said, "That gentleman ahead of us was a cop, and a damned good one. He went plainclothes early in his career, and racked up a list of arrests and convictions that was staggering—especially since he didn't confine himself to assigned cases. Problem was, he couldn't cultivate the habit of turning his head at the right moments. Kept arresting the wrong people. His superiors started losing kickbacks and payoffs, so they trumped up a charge and fired him. Long hired him before I and a few other executives of federal organizations could get our hands on him."

"Oh," Kelsey said a little blankly.

Hagen went on, still conversational. "The lawyer— Rafferty Lewis—was an assistant district attorney at a ridiculously young age. He, too, had a problem playing political games. Long hired him, ostensibly to handle his legal affairs. He and his partner do that of course. But Lewis is also a dollar-a-year man for the government. He's done some work for the Justice Department, and has been in on a couple of crime commissions. He's a pilot, and holds a sharpshooter rating with all handguns. He's also extraordinarily cool under pressure, and has an ability to fit himself into any situation he encounters. Gets about as nervous as a bag of cement."

"Ummm," Kelsey said thoughtfully.

"And Zachary Steele," Hagen said dryly, "is an army all by himself. He was with the Special Forces in 'Nam—lied about his age to get in. Unlike a lot of big men, he's *stronger* than he looks, and he's as fast as a rattlesnake. Brilliant too; he has an amazing memory, and a sixth sense when it comes to codes and intelligence work. He's an electronics genius; there isn't a security system in existence he couldn't crack."

There was a long silence, and then Kelsey said "Um" again, adding, "Objection withdrawn."

Hagen smiled at his cigar. "You made copies of the tapes?"

"Of course," Kelsey replied, mildly offended. "That bug on Raven's bracelet works perfectly. We get ready to move?"

"We," Hagen said, "get ready to move."

Raven knew that Josh would come to the penthouse again that night. She turned on the tape player as soon as she got inside, and then went to wash away the ice maiden in the shower. She removed her bracelet and placed it in a dresser drawer, then undressed and removed her makeup before stepping into the stall. Luxuriating in the hot spray, she was curiously not surprised when a draft of cool air heralded an arrival. Turning in the roomy stall, she pushed wet hair out of her eyes and smiled.

"I locked the door," she murmured.

Josh shut the stall door to enclose them within. "I've been taking lessons from Zach," he said breathlessly, reaching for her. "I picked the lock."

Hot water streamed over them as he pulled her close, and his gaze was fixed on her face. Remembering the hours without her, he groaned. "Forever. It's been forever—"

Raven's arms went around his neck and her mouth was eager beneath his, hungry. The mat of hair on his chest scraped her breasts sensuously and her legs moved to twine with his. She could feel his hands moving slowly over the slippery flesh of her back, spanning her waist, lowering to cup her hips. And her head fell back when his mouth left hers to taste her throat, her shoulders.

He lifted her against him, the slide of their bodies an electric caress, and his lips found the hard, throbbing tips of her breasts. She tasted sweet and clean from the soap and felt vibrantly alive, and the steam within the shower enclosed them in a hot, wet, intimate blanket of sensation.

Blindly, Josh reached for the faucet, turning the water off. He opened the stall and stepped out, bringing her with him, reaching for towels. And, just as it had been that morning, he was fascinated to watch her flesh change as it was dried. Sleek, shiny wetness became satin smoothness as he moved the terry-cloth over her skin. She was flushed from the heat of the shower, her body rosy, her eyes darkened, aroused. He knelt before her to dry her glorious long legs, pressing a warm kiss on the silky skin beside her navel.

He rose to his feet, wrapping her in a towel and knotting one around his own waist, then led her out to the dressing table and began drying her hair. This, too, was lovemaking; the slow, sensuous movements of the brush through her hair kept them both intent, absorbed. And not until her hair was black silk gleaming with a thousand highlights did Josh turn off the dryer and set it and the brush aside.

Towels were flung to the floor, and the bed, covers pulled back, cushioned them in cool softness.

Raven's fingers locked in his still-damp hair, and she met his mouth fiercely, glorying in the hard strength of his body against hers.

There was a curious difference in their lovemaking. Both had spent long hours apart tormented by tension and memories of this bed. And with the intimacy they had found here had come a far more intense awareness of the dangers facing them. They were powerfully, acutely, sensitive to every touch, every glance, every murmured endearment.

Desire coiled and writhed, a living thing caged by flesh, a starving, demanding thing existing only to be sated. It took control of them, drove them wildly to lose themselves in its rich, potent texture.

If Raven had once hesitated to lose herself in feeling, there was so such barrier now. She wanted him, needed him; the hard planes of his body intrigued her, obsessed her. Her hands stroked his back, feathering lightly down his spine in a caress that made him shudder. She traced his shoulders and arms, explored his lean ribs and powerful chest, fascinated. Her mouth found the tight hardness of his nipples, and heat moved strongly in her loins at the taste and feel of him.

She twined her legs about his, absorbed by the caress of his hair-rough flesh, moved oddly when every touch shook his powerful body with increasing need. His hoarse mutters of encouragement fueled her intense desire to touch him, explore him, and she became engrossed in the body so wonderfully different from her own.

Every breath Josh drew was fire in his lungs, and he felt as if she were tearing him apart with her soft hands and warm mouth, tearing him apart and then making him whole again, and again, and again. It was torture, a sweet, mindless torture that he wouldn't have stopped even if death promised to follow.

He was no stranger to passion, but this went far beyond anything he'd ever known before. This was raw, essential need, profound in its power, and just this side of madness.

He was starving for her with a hunger that was voracious, shattering his control, and Josh pulled her back up beside him with a hoarse cry, moving over her, sinking his body into hers with a power that strove to make them one, fused. The inferno inside him was burning out of control, and her equally wild response only fed the flames, searing them both.

Her body strained against his, trembling, her soft cries pushing his desperate need almost over the edge. He felt the sharp sting of her nails in his back, felt the silken touch of her thighs about his hips. Her body sheathed his in a velvet clasp that sent violent shivers of hot ecstasy along his spine, and it still wasn't enough, he still didn't have enough of her.

There was no time for gentleness, no desire for it. In the shared desperation of their need they were matched, their bodies moving instantly into a savage rhythm. Tension built strongly, winding tighter and tighter, hot and powerful.

Raven cried out wildly when tension shattered in a hot explosion, feeling her body hold him tightly, pleasure washing over her in mindless waves. She felt as well as heard his hoarse cry, felt him shudder in the shock waves of his release.

His trembling body was heavy on hers, but Raven held him cradled and refused to give him up. She smoothed the damp flesh of his shoulders and back, feeling his lips moving against her shoulder, her throat.

"Oh, Raven, my Raven." His voice was a breath of sound, drained, awed. He lifted his head, gazing down into her eyes with his own, dark, still turbulent. "I knew you were out there somewhere . . . and I was *worried* about this?"

She remembered, then, a dark and handsome man on the floor at her feet, staring up at her with dazed, rueful eyes. "You said something like that the first night," she murmured. "I thought you were concussed."

"I know what you thought." He kissed her, easing up on his elbows to lessen the weight on her. "But I wasn't. It's just that I've always known I'd fall in love with a beautiful brunette someday— and lose control. Scared the hell out of me." He kissed her again, slowly, deeply.

Raven was a little puzzled, amused. "How could you possibly know that?"

"Beats me. But I did. Why do you suppose I've surrounded myself with blondes all these years?"

"Practice?" she suggested dryly.

He chuckled. "That did sound arrogant, didn't it? It wasn't meant that way. I went out with blondes because not one of them ever made me lose control. But you do. . . . Dear Lord, you do, sweetheart. I can't stop looking at you, touching you. And every time we make love, the feelings just keep growing stronger."

She pushed a lock of his dark hair back, gazing into his warm blue eyes. "I love you," she whispered. "I didn't know it could be like this. I never even dreamed I could feel this way."

Josh rolled suddenly until he lay on his back

with her on top of him, his hands moving over her in a gentle caress. "I love you," he murmured. "You'll never know how much."

For one wild, passionate moment, Raven wanted to ask him to take her away somewhere. To a place with no shadows, no dangers, no knife-edge parts to play. Then the spurt of desperation faded, and she knew that neither of them would want that, even if it was a choice offered to them.

Exhaustion claimed her slowly, and she was only dimly aware that he had managed to pull the covers up around them. Warm in the security he gave her, she listened to his heart beating steadily beneath her cheek.

And there were no nightmares.

Seven

Frowning, Zach paced around the living room. He returned finally to the computer printout spread on the coffee table, sitting down on the couch and staring worriedly at the papers.

Josh, beginning to look strained all the time now, had gone off hours earlier to spend another night in Raven's penthouse apartment, and Zach worried about that too. Not so much because of the danger inherent in the action—although there was, of course, very real danger—but because of the effect on his friend that was growing more visible with every passing day. Though Josh had said nothing about it to any of his men, Zach could see only too clearly that the situation was becoming intolerable; this was something Josh could not control, and it had been that way from the beginning.

Zach had a strong feeling that Raven, though clearly in love with Josh, was unwilling to make a commitment while danger threatened them both.

And Zach wished fervently that he could have just five minutes alone with her to explain why that decision, though a reasonable and natural one certainly, was entirely wrong for Josh.

Why, in fact, it was tearing him apart.

But Zach knew better than to interfere. Josh and Raven would have to work it out by themselves—if they could without tearing each other to shreds. Zach's only certainty was that both Josh and Raven were the rare type of human who met life head-on and wrestled fiercely to get what they wanted and needed; and both were perceptive, courageous people.

If a solution was possible, they would find it between themselves.

If there was time.

He sighed, staring down at the printout. A worry he could do nothing about. And this bothered him too. He had a vague, unsettled feeling that they were being manipulated, pawns on some ridiculous, larger-than-life chessboard in a game played for some unseen person's perverse enjoyment. He ran fingers through his dark hair, frowning. It didn't make sense, dammit, it just *didn't*.

"You're still up?" Rafferty came into the room from his own, yawning and tying the belt of his robe absently. "It's almost dawn, for God's sake."

Zach grunted. "Well, why're you up then?"

"The traditional remedy for insomnia. Cocoa." Rafferty went to the bar and poured a generous measure of brandy into a snifter. "Or the modern version."

"Make it two, will you?" Zach was silent until the snifter was in his hand and a swallow burned its way gently down his throat. "Thanks."

Rafferty sank into a chair and glanced at the printout spread on the table. "I consider this a part of last night rather than this morning," he announced with a mild attempt to satisfy the dictates of convention, sipping his drink. "Besides, the sun must be over the yardarm *somewhere.*" Then he noticed Zach's lack of attention. "You're still going over that stuff?"

Zach nodded, then said, "It's been a couple of days since Travers told Raven he'd make the arrangements, right?"

"According to Josh."

"So it could be today."

"Or tomorrow. Or next week. Who knows?"

"Comforting bastard, aren't you?"

After a moment, Rafferty sighed. "All right, so I'm worried too. He looked like hell when he left, didn't he? I guess we all should have known if Josh ever lost that obsessive control, he'd be in trouble. Well, he's in trouble. And there's not a damned thing any of us can do about it. Not us."

Zach stirred uneasily. "I know. But . . . He's too near the edge to explain himself to her—and she's the only one who could help him. If they could meet openly, it might be different, he might be able to handle it."

"I don't know." Rafferty shook his head a little. "Look at what he's been through. I'm still surprised he managed to pull himself up after you handed him that printout. From what you told us, it almost killed him. And he hasn't had a chance to get his balance back."

Staring down at the papers, Zach said slowly, "Yeah. He hardly needs something else on his plate right now. Which is why I really don't want to hit him with this."

"With what?" Rafferty leaned forward.

Zach picked up a pencil and began checking names, dates, places, occurrences. "Look at this. Here. And here . . ."

"How did you get this?" Josh traced the faint scar on her lower back.

It was early morning. Raven was sitting on the edge of the bed, preparing to rise. Her long hair was swept around over one shoulder, leaving the graceful line of her spine bare. She was still for a moment, then looked back over her shoulder at him. Lightly and casually, she said, "The cavalry didn't arrive fast enough once."

Josh sat up slowly, and his hand moved around to her stomach, pulling her back against his chest. "What?" he asked unsteadily, something cold and sick inside him. He had hoped the thin scar had an innocent, ordinary explanation: she had fallen out of a tree when she was six . . . had a car accident . . . tripped on some stairs. . . .

Her hand covered his, and Raven leaned her head back on his shoulder. Her voice was quiet. "It was a kidnapping case. I'd found where they were holding the victim and called for backup. I had a directional microphone, and I heard them discussing the little girl. They were bored, and they wanted to . . . Anyway, I couldn't wait. I climbed up to the window of the room where they were holding her and managed to get her out, unfortunately not before they heard. The backup arrived, but not quite fast enough." Her laugh was a little shaky. "I was lucky the kidnapper didn't have a gun handy."

Both of Josh's arms were around her now, and he held her tightly. The warm, feminine curves of her body pressed against him, and she felt too delicate, too fragile, to have fought for her life with a man holding a knife. "I don't ever want you hurt," he said in a thick, impeded voice.

Her cheek rubbed against his jaw for a moment, and she said softly, "That's something you can't stop, Josh. Life hurts; you know that as well as I do."

His arms tightened and he kissed her shoulder, looking down at her full, thrusting breasts. Her shining black hair fell over one mound in a silky curtain, and he brushed the curtain aside with his fingertips, searching out the satin of her skin. His hands moved, surrounding warm flesh, his thumbs teasing. He saw as well as heard her sigh as he gazed intently at her nipples, tightening, becoming hard points of desire.

Watching her instant response drove his own constant desire higher and higher, but this time his mind refused to let go of worry, unease. Fear. She was so elusive . . . and not his. Never, somehow, his. Something dark moved deeply within him. His eyes remained fixed on her, his fingers moved gently, and he heard his voice as if from a great distance.

"You're so guarded . . . and so hurt inside. I can feel it. Sometimes I see it in your eyes." His lips brushed her shoulder, the warm hollow at the base of her throat. "It tears me apart to see you hurting."

Raven fought to control her body's response to him, dimly aware that what he was telling her was important, vitally important, that she should try to listen to more than his words, try to hear what his rough voice was telling her. But her body was mastered by desire, her mind seduced. Heat tingled and writhed within her, spreading outward from the hollowness that throbbed emptily for him.

"You hide from me," he murmured hoarsely, one hand slipping down over her flat, quivering stomach. "Except when you're like this. Except when you want me. Then you let yourself go."

"Josh . . ."

He shuddered. "Even your voice changes . . . warm and soft and wanting. And your incredible eyes lose that guarded brightness and go so dark, so deep." Abruptly, he pulled her back onto the bed, raising himself beside her to nuzzle his face between her breasts. "And you touch me then," he whispered as her hands rose to stroke his shoulders. "Only then. You never touch me unless you want me. You don't draw back when I touch you, but you don't touch me. Only when you want me. Only when we've made love and your defenses are still down."

The slight rasp of his morning beard against her breasts was driving her crazy, and Raven couldn't think of anything but his touch. The touch that ignited her. No matter how many times they made love, she was seduced again and again by desire, ignited, flaming with need for him.

One of her legs was pinned by his, and she moved the other to tangle with his long, powerful ones, stroking her flesh against his, catching her breath, feeling the flames rise. She shifted restlessly, trying to draw him closer, frustrated when his resistance defeated her.

He breathed hotly on one yearning nipple, flicked it with his tongue maddeningly. "I can make you forget everything but me and what we do to each other," he whispered. "I can always do that. Can't I, Raven?"

"Josh—" She gasped, trying to pull his head down, desperate to feel his mouth on her throbbing flesh.

"Can't I?" His voice hardened. "Tell me!"

Dazed, she stared into that lean, hard, almost cruel face, its handsome lines altered by something old and driven. His eyes were bright with a sheen of determination and a nerve throbbed erratically at one corner of his mouth like a living thing writhing in torment.

Raven had believed that she'd seen the different facets of his personality. She'd seen his humor, his consideration, his strength and power; she'd seen his gentleness and passion and a desire as wild as unreason. She had seen his anger. She had never seen this.

But she recognized it.

"Tell me, Raven." His tongue moved teasingly, and one hand slipped down over her stomach while his leg parted hers in a single strong, irresistible movement. His face was hard, intent, his eyes almost blind.

Even as her body responded instantly, inexorably, to his erotic touch, Raven held on fiercely to a shred of awareness, of understanding. All her instincts told her that if she didn't understand what he was doing and why he was driven to do it, it could destroy them both.

He was something beyond himself, she realized, lost, torn from his moorings by primitive, utterly male needs. And she had done that to him. Elusive and enigmatic because her life often depended on it, she had unwittingly driven him to this place, where he was desperate, trapped.

He was a man who had known light romantic and sexual conquests, secure in his control, sure of himself. The thought of falling in love and losing control of his life had "scared the hell" out of him, and he had flinched from that with what amounted to an obsession.

She remembered the file on him in a flash, recalled all the unrelated facts that she now knew were tied inextricably together. His brilliant business maneuvering, the tactics complex but always within his control. The security force built carefully around him to provide a maximum amount of control in any given situation. The long succession of blondes casually escorted, never the same more than a couple of times and none allowed close enough to challenge his control of his life.

In his childhood, events had occurred beyond his control, stealing first his father's life and then his mother's, gifting him with almost unimaginable wealth and power, setting him apart from other boys, other men. And from those events, he had wrenched control, guarding himself against further pain, mapping his life with the sure touch of caution.

Then, in a single moment, he had lost that guarded, necessary control. He had, against all odds and perhaps his own nature, fallen in love—and his carefully planned path had taken an abrupt and unnerving turn. If theirs had been a normal romance, Josh would have coped, if not easily, then at least without this terrible struggle. But normality was the last thing they had found.

Danger hovered darkly in their present, and each had walked through a past filled with painful, hazardous shadows. Their time together was not even their own—stolen, furtive, hurried. Desperate. At any moment they could be torn apart, perhaps forever, the ground beneath them treacherously uncertain.

And Josh, control snatched from his grasp, had struggled violently to cope. To regain a thread of control. He had coped—somehow—with the devastating possibility that the woman he loved was something evil, emerging from that struggle with trust intact, belief strong. He had coped with the reality of her double life, never asking her to walk away from what she felt she had to do. He had coped with the dangers she faced, shaken by them but unflinching, struggling constantly and visibly against the male instinct to guard and protect.

He had loved her without reservation, giving of himself freely, asking of her only what she would give with equal freedom.

And Raven, unthinking, had held back. Unaware of the conflict tearing him apart, she had not realized what she was doing to him by protecting herself. Guarded, wary, she was unwilling to risk her innermost self, the hidden soul she fought to keep strong in spite of scars, because it was very nearly all that was real to her in her life.

She didn't know, even now, why the tenuous, hard-won thread of Josh's control had finally snapped. Perhaps it had been the visible scar of her past crying out the dangers she had faced. Perhaps it had been a sense of time running out, of risk and uncertainty closing around them with dark talons. Perhaps it had been all of that. Whatever the cause, the deeply ingrained instincts that had built an obsession demanded that Josh assert the only control he could hope to win. Male instincts millions of years old demanded that he take, possess, brand her indelibly as his. He had to find certainty in her, because there was no other certainty possible now.

And if he did that, battered down her guards against her will and took from her what she resisted giving, what he took would destroy her— and him, when he was sane again.

"Tell me!" he ordered in a raw, harsh tone, his strong body tense and hard, his mouth moving in hot, savage demand over her flesh. "Tell me that I can make you forget until nothing else matters. Tell me."

Awareness, understanding flowed through Raven swiftly then. Even torn in two, he was not violent, and she wasn't afraid of him. But she knew her response to his needs now would either bond them fierily together or tear them apart for all time. Words she should have given him before now would not be enough, she knew. Not now. Not enough to stop him, not enough to drain the brutal need from his soul.

To give him the certainty he needed, she would have to submerge herself, lose herself totally, offer everything she was to him. It was nothing so simple and basic as lovemaking, nothing so easy as the joining of two bodies. What he needed was an utter and complete release of all inhibitions, all restraints, all awareness of anything and everything but the total satisfaction of the raging emotions between them.

She had to tear away her pride, her instincts of

self-preservation, lose her sense of self before he blindly, desperately, ripped them away himself.

Her choice was made in an instant, a heartbeat.

She moved against his roughly caressing hands, her own tangling in his hair, demanding an end to his torturing. "Yes," she said, and her tone was harsh, too, and wild, breaking away from her because she wasn't herself anymore. "You make me forget. Nothing matters but you."

"Tell me what you want," he commanded, lifting his head to stare down at her with glittering eyes. His fingers probed with sure knowledge.

Raven moaned, the whimpering animal sound surging up from her deepest being. Restraints were snapping one by one, leaving her a primitive, hungering creature with no mind, no awareness of anything but the needs of her body and soul. His knowing fingers were stroking her intimately, insistently, and her hips lifted to the touch. "You!" she gasped, her nails digging into his back, her body writhing. "I want you . . . all of you. . . ." Her voice was strained, trembling.

The aching, burning tip of her breast was drawn into his hungry mouth, his tongue swirling. He caught her wrists in one hand and held them above her head in an inescapable but painless grip, his other hand increasing its erotic caresses. And when she convulsed against him, her body arching and a wild cry torn from her throat, he lifted his head to watch her fixedly, still caressing her, driving her higher, refusing to allow her the downward slide into peace.

Again and again he shattered her senses, catching her mindless cries in his mouth, denying himself release. He held her still when she would have moved violently, resisted when she sought to free her arms and pull him closer. He fed her hunger, yet left her empty and aching, needing him with an all-consuming craving that turned her nerves to fire.

And when he finally moved between her thighs, she could only shiver wildly and cradle his body, her freed arms reaching to enfold him, her strong legs lifting, twining about him. Her voice was a shaking, helpless plea, wordless, primal. He drove into her with a single rough thrust, his hard body filling the emptiness that ached for him until she could feel him throbbing deep within her, and her cry was a sound of triumph.

For Josh, the world had condensed, shrunk, tunneled until it contained only them. His only conscious awareness was of her, her body sheathing his so tightly, so softly, her shaking voice uttering cries that drove him crazy, her nails digging into his back in sharp stings of desire. The inferno within his own body was a crucible, melting away everything but the savage hunger driving him.

He was still for an eternal moment, holding himself deep inside her, so close to exploding he could feel the feathery tremors along every taut nerve of his body. She moaned deeply, raggedly, her inner muscles contracting around him in a sudden, ecstatic rhythm, and he buried his face in her throat, gritting his teeth, hanging on to control for the fierce pleasure of feeling her release so intimately.

But his body, desperate, assumed a rhythm of its own. He caught her breathless cries, his mouth wild and hot on hers, driving into her with the strength and power of lost control and mindless need. She was taking him, all of him, and the satiny clasp of her body eagerly fueled the explosion both demanded.

His body shuddered violently as he drove himself into her, unbearable tension snapping and sending shock waves jolting through him in a feeling light years beyond pleasure. He was dying . . . he was intensely, vividly alive . . . torn in half by the violent clash of life and death and the satisfaction of a hunger too primitive to have a name.

He lay heavily on her, his chest moving with the deep, ragged breaths his exhausted body demanded, his face buried in her neck. Raven held him with what strength she had left to her, stroking the powerful, glistening muscles of his back with hands that shook uncontrollably.

There was more, this time, than a simple sense of wellbeing. She felt almost electrified, acutely alive, and there were no shadows within her. For the first time in her life she had given herself totally, completely, stripping away the layers guarding her inner self and exposing what she was to the searing, healing touch of his need—and her own.

She slid one hand up his spine, threading her fingers through his thick black hair, and with a new and curiously powerful sense of communication, she knew the instant he came back to himself, became aware again. "I love you," she murmured, her breath warm against his shoulder.

Josh lifted his head, his breath catching as he looked at her. Her eyes were wide and dark and bottomless, glowing with an inner fire far too deep and strong ever to be hidden by an enigmatic surface of violet or an expert shading of makeup.

He eased up on his elbows, shaken by what he saw and by what he had so nearly done to them. If she had resisted him . . . Memories like primal growls in the back of his throat haunted him, tautening a body that trembled from the strain of what he was feeling. "Raven . . ." His hands found her face, shaking. "I could have hurt you." He remembered the savagery of his desire, the driven strength, and closed his eyes. "I did hurt you."

She lifted her head from the pillow, kissing him very tenderly. "You didn't hurt me. You could never hurt me," she murmured. "Don't you think I know that?"

He was still too shaken, too unnerved by his descent into a dark and savage place to be reassured. "I wanted . . . my God, I wanted everything. I didn't think about hurting you, only about taking you. Making sure you belonged to me."

Raven didn't think now, she only responded to the anguish in his voice. Softly, her voice husky, she said, "There was something cold in me, something dark and alone. It isn't there anymore, Josh. There was a wound so deep, the light could never reach it, never heal it. But you did."

He looked at her, gazed deep into those bottomless, darkly flaming eyes, and saw truth. Whatever had happened between them, Raven's need had been as great as his own, and the certainty both had required now lay deeply, warmly, within them.

"I love you," he said, his voice a bare thread of sound. "I love you so much."

• • •

She had promised to meet Leon Travers for lunch, and Josh, dressed, watched as she sat at the dressing table and piled her long hair atop her head and secured it expertly with a few pins. She was wearing a silk dress of deep, shimmering violet. And her eyes, even with the careful shading of makeup, were no longer cool and enigmatic.

The changes wrought in her would never again be disguised by a part she played. Her eyes were inexplicably wider, more vivid, and stirringly *alive.* No shadows lurked there, no hints of cool disinterest.

Josh got to his feet and went to stand behind her. "If you ever allow anyone but me to watch you dress and put on makeup," he said casually, "I will strangle you."

Laughter shimmered instantly to life in the eyes that met his in the mirror. "Oh, really?"

"Yes." His hands lifted to her shoulders, moving gently to feel the beloved flesh and bone, the compelling warmth of her. "I never thought about it before, but there's something very intimate in watching a woman get ready to go out." His hands swept over the silk and surrounded her neck warmly. "Makes a man feel possessive."

Raven gazed at the reflection of his face, seeing an easing of the strain that had gripped it for so many days. He was curiously at peace now, something she could feel as well as see. She reached up to catch his hands, leaning her head back against him with little thought of her hairstyle. "I'm not objecting," she whispered.

"Good, because I can't seem to handle it rationally," he said, bending to kiss her lightly. Then he moved away, a gleam in his eyes warning her that if they lingered, she'd certainly be late for her appointment.

Very late.

Tearing her gaze from that silent, hot promise, Raven took a last assessing look into the mirror and frowned slightly. She started to reach for the small case of eyeshadow, but his comment stopped her.

"It won't work."

She turned on the low stool, staring up at him in puzzlement. "Why not?"

Unable to keep his hands off her, Josh brushed his knuckles lightly beneath her chin, caressing the silky flesh. "Because you've changed," he said quietly, watching for her reaction. "Your eyes have come alive—really alive. You can't disguise them with makeup any longer."

She looked at him for a long moment, then smiled suddenly. "You've ruined me for Hagen," she said, sounding pleased. Then she laughed. "I'll just have to keep my lashes lowered demurely, I suppose, or wear sunglasses in the restaurant."

Josh took her hands and pulled her gently to her feet. "Travers will see," he said, uneasy as the import of that hit him. "He'll know you're different, know something's happened."

"I'll think of something to tell him. Don't worry." She kissed his chin. "Now, I've got to get the bracelet, so be quiet." She had told him earlier about the microphone in her bracelet, which had reassured him somewhat regarding Hagen's precautions.

Instead of allowing her to move away instantly, Josh caught her chin and turned her face up, kissing her deeply and thoroughly with the new possessiveness that had marked them both.

Raven melted against him, drawing strength from him, glorying in the feeling of belonging to him. It was a special kind of belonging, she had decided, something deep and sure, with no overtones of mastery or selfishness. They belonged to each other, and both were more than they had been.

"I love you," he murmured.

She smiled, her fingers touching his lips with a sense of wonder. "I love you." Reluctantly, she went to get her bracelet and capture her now elusive alter ego.

Then they left, she to travel down in the elevator, her aloof expression and dark glasses hiding the glow within, he to vanish discreetly out the back way, unseen and unheard.

Rafferty looked up from the desk as Josh came into the suite, and he went still as his sharp eyes absorbed the change. *Well, now,* he thought. *Well, now.*

"You guys had lunch?" Josh asked briskly, dropping his car keys on the table near the door and coming into the room to sink down in a comfortable chair.

"No." Zach, his printout put away, was also intent on studying changes.

Smiling quite unconsciously, Josh propped his feet on the coffee table. "Room service isn't too bad," he remarked idly.

After a moment, Zach looked at Rafferty. "He imports the finest chef he can get from Europe, then says the food isn't bad. You want to remind him he's in his own hotel, or should I?"

Rafferty's laugh changed into a cough by the time mildly surprised blue eyes looked his way. "It's your hotel, Josh," he ventured.

"I know that." Josh looked from one to the other, coming to the conclusion, finally, that Raven hadn't been the only one outwardly changed. Curiously enough, he wasn't in the least embarrassed or self-conscious. "If I've grown another head," he said politely, "somebody tell me. I'll need to buy more hats."

"You don't wear hats," Zach murmured.

Josh looked at him.

Rafferty cleared his throat hastily. "Room service sounds fine. Where's the menu?"

"I'll get it." Zach rose from the couch with the uncanny grace that was surprising in so big a man, going over to the bar, where the menu lay.

"Where's Lucas?" Josh asked absently.

Zach, turning from the bar and behind Josh, sent Rafferty a quick look and slightly shook his head.

After an imperceptible pause, the lawyer answered in a casual tone. "Oh, he had some errands. Probably be back before room service gets here, though."

"We'll order for him, then," Josh said, accepting the menu from Zach.

Rafferty spoke slowly. "Josh, it could be today, couldn't it?"

Some strain returned to Josh's face, but not nearly as much as they were accustomed to seeing. "Could. But Raven says if Travers sticks to his usual method, it'll be at night. Tomorrow night is the most likely."

"Will she know where she's going?" Zach asked.

"Not until she gets there." Josh stared at the menu, and something grim, determined, tightened his face for a brief moment, then was gone.

Zach glanced at the lawyer, and Rafferty nodded with a resignation Josh didn't see.

Both of them had known all along.

Hagen and Kelsey sat in a car a block from an elegant restaurant and ate their lunch from various paper and Styrofoam containers. Kelsey crumpled up the wrapping of his hamburger and said gloomily, "She did that deliberately, the witch." He gestured to the small device that was currently giving them an ear inside the restaurant. "She told us exactly what she was having for lunch, *knowing* we'd be stuck out here eating flavored paper."

"Undoubtedly," Hagen agreed, staring with some disfavor at his own meal.

The conversation going on inside ended for the time being as Raven excused herself, and Kelsey sent a thoughtful look at his boss. "Eight years, and this is the first time I've known you to get involved enough to share a stakeout."

"Big fish," Hagen said dryly. "And this is one I intend to catch."

"Thanks."

Hagen chuckled. "No offense intended, my boy. You're a good operative, possibly one of my best. So is Raven. You know, of course, that this will be her final assignment?"

Kelsey sighed. "Yeah, I guessed. Long. Well, I grudge him the best partner I've ever had, but I'm glad he can make her happy."

There was silence for a few moments, until Raven returned to the table inside the restaurant. Kelsey, listening, cocked his head to one side intently.

"What?" Hagen asked.

"He sounds a little tense, don't you think?"

Hagen listened to the conversation, which was a casual one. "I don't hear it."

Kelsey shook his head, still vaguely bothered. "Must be getting punchy from all this flavored paper," he muttered. "Additives and numbered dyes and . . . whatever. Affecting what I fondly call my mind."

Hagen looked at him for a moment, then returned his attention to the conversation. "Could be," he said almost to himself.

In the garage level of the soaring hotel, Lucas Kendrick paused in the shadows to gaze around intently. Convinced he was alone in the echoing place, he moved forward silently until he stood beside a rental car.

Ever since a crazed ex-employee in Miami had traced Josh through his rental car and had taken a wild shot at him some years before, they had learned to take no chances. Rental cars were always logged as being serviced while they were in his possession. Even when Josh drove one of his own cars, the plates were switched erratically.

Lucas was in and out of the car quickly and silently, and left nothing behind him except a small device hidden securely under the dashboard.

Eight

Josh was agitated during the early part of the afternoon, relaxing somewhat only after Raven called him from a pay phone in the ladies' rest room of the restaurant to report that Leon had canceled their dinner date for the evening. It seemed to indicate clearly that it was not yet "arranged" for Raven to see the girls she proposed to acquire for the international interests she was supposed to represent.

"So it's not tonight?"

Josh looked at Rafferty as he hung up the phone and shrugged—as much to ease tense shoulders as anything else. "Looks that way. With any luck, it'll be tomorrow night." To himself, he added, "Then it'll be over."

Rafferty said nothing, but watched as Josh rose and moved around the room absently. He remained silent when his friend and employer suddenly returned to his desk and opened a drawer, pulling out a shoulder harness containing a rather deadly looking automatic. Josh removed the clip from the gun and checked it, his expression still abstracted, then replaced it and shrugged into the harness.

Lucas entered the room just then, and unlike Rafferty, he chose not to keep silent. "Is it to-night?" he asked quickly.

"No."

"Then, why—?" Lucas gestured toward the gun Josh now wore comfortably, as if it were a part of him.

Josh frowned a little. Still frowning, he shrugged. "I don't know. Just a feeling." When the phone rang, he made no move to answer, but stood star-ing out the window.

Rafferty got up and answered it, then held out the receiver to Josh. "Serena."

His expression lightening, Josh took the receiver and spoke into it with mock severity. "You can't have it."

"Have what, Josh?" His half-sister's voice held its usual soft, serene, deceptively unthreatening tone.

"Whatever it is you want. Money, probably. Why don't you con your husband into handing over large sums for your various projects? I happen to know Brian isn't exactly poor."

"Josh, have you been drinking?"

He could hardly help but grin at the gentle ques-tion. "No, Rena, I haven't been drinking. Did you call for a reason, or just to brighten my day?"

"Curiosity. Daddy said you called to ask him about Hagen. What're you up to, Josh?"

"You *know* Hagen?"

"Well, I know of him, of course. Daddy says he's

absolutely brilliant, totally devoted to law and order, and as twisty as snakes in a barrel."

Josh reflected that he really shouldn't be surprised at Serena's knowledge. She had, after all, grown up much nearer than himself to the secretive world Stuart Jameson inhabited; she would certainly be aware of all the players in that particular game.

"Josh?"

He stirred. "Yes, he told me the same thing."

Patiently, she said, "I know that. What I *want* to know is why you asked about him."

Somewhat belatedly, Josh wondered if his phone might be tapped. He knew that Zach took precautions wherever they stayed, but wasn't certain if that included more than a daily check on the phone. He looked up to ask Rafferty or Lucas, but found that both men had silently left the room to give him privacy.

Cautiously, he told his sister, "This isn't a good time to talk about it, Rena."

She was nothing if not quick; her voice didn't change, but he knew she understood. "Later, then. What I *really* called to ask about was your brunette."

She could, Josh realized, still surprise him. "Um . . . what brunette?"

"The one who finally caught you." Serena was patient. "That's why you're still in L.A., isn't it?"

Josh cleared his throat, torn between laughter and resignation. "Well, as a matter of fact . . ."

Her soft laughter was warm and rich. "It finally happened, didn't it? You got swept right off your feet!"

Remembering, Josh laughed as well. "You're more right than you know. And how the hell—?"

"Josh, you haven't interrupted a business trip—except that time for me—in years! Besides, I've been watching the papers, and you haven't appeared with a blonde on your arm since you got there. I know you. Such a radical break in your habits has *got* to mean—"

"All right, all right." He reminded himself again that the phone could be tapped, annoyed by the need to guard his words. "If it weren't for Brian's tendency to go berserk when someone lays an unkind hand on you, you'd probably be burned at the stake, witch. My only solace is that you had nothing to do with my meeting Raven."

"What a wonderful name! Josh, when can we meet her?"

His throat abruptly closed up, and Josh swallowed the lump. "Soon, I hope."

After a slight pause, she said, "Can I help?"

"No." He cleared his throat, not surprised by her perceptiveness. "No, honey, but thanks."

"Well, I'm here."

"Yes. Say hello to Brian for me."

"I will."

He cradled the receiver gently, staring at it, remembering for the first time in years the pact he and Serena had made as kids. It was now an ingrained habit both observed, and he, at least, never thought about it. Until now.

They never said good-bye, not even casually, when any distance separated them.

Staring at the phone, Josh thought about that. A pact concocted between two children, born in the darkest hours of their young lives when tragedy had stolen their mother and locked them within a cage of "security" designed to protect them. Stuart, silent and shattered, had withdrawn temporarily from his daughter and stepson, and they had clung to one another in bewildered pain, understanding only that there were things they could not control, could not change.

From that common experience, each had strengthened the innate traits they shared. Serena, brilliant and loving, had evolved a method of controlling her life that was as devious as it was natural for her. She schemed and plotted, arranging situations to suit her, always uncannily accurate in reading people and their reactions to her plots.

Josh, older than she and more cynical, had taken a direct route in an effort to control his own destiny. Certain deep within himself that he would love a brunette, he had simply avoided women with dark hair—obsessively avoided them. He gathered about him an impressive force of intelligence and security people, preferring to be aware of possible dangers, avoiding surprises of any kind. He grimly learned to recognize what he had referred to Raven as "the dark side of the streets," knowing that threats came from there.

And now . . .

He stared at the phone, realizing that some scars never really healed. Raven would never forget her sister. And he and Serena would never bring themselves to say good-bye to each other, because there was, somewhere within them, still two young kids stubbornly telling themselves that if they didn't say good-bye . . . neither of them could go away forever.

He realized only then that he had never said good-bye to Raven.

Raven couldn't have said exactly what was bothering her. She had been a little worried that Leon would see the change in her and react somehow, but he very obviously had not. And she soon forgot that worry, vaguely disturbed by something in Leon's manner.

All during lunch, he had been his usual urbane self, talking casually, as he normally did. Apologetically, he had canceled their evening plans, explaining that there were some overseas calls he had to make. His expression and gaze were unreadable as always, his voice courteous.

But Raven had seen the slightest indication of restlessness or some similar emotion in him. He had toyed with his wineglass, his napkin. He had eaten little and glanced at his watch more than once. All uncharacteristic of Leon Travers.

She had the strong but inexplicable feeling that he barely knew she was with him, that his mind was far away.

Very uncharacteristic.

Raven had taken a chance and called Josh, wanting him to know they could be together earlier than usual that night. But she had been a little distracted, even while talking to him, still bothered by nothing she could put a finger on.

All her instincts were screaming at her, and she didn't know *why*.

Talking casually to Leon, keeping her cool mask in place but avoiding any direct look at him that could show him she had changed, Raven devoted a tiny, analytical part of her mind to the problem.

What was wrong? *What?*

Zach came in minutes after Josh had finished his call. He looked at the gun, but said nothing.

"Is this phone safe?" Josh asked.

"Yes," Zach answered simply, not surprised by the question. "And we haven't been bugged. I check twice a day."

"Good." Josh stirred, then got to his feet and drew on his jacket. "I'm going to the penthouse; Raven doesn't have to see Travers tonight."

"Why the gun?"

Josh walked across the room and picked up his car keys, finally replying shortly, "I don't know." The door closed softly behind him.

Within a minute, Zach had rousted Lucas and Rafferty from their rooms, and the three men stood together near the desk.

"He wore the damned gun, didn't he," Rafferty said gloomily, and it wasn't a question.

Zach didn't waste a nod. "He's bothered by something. Maybe Raven sounded tense or worried when they talked, I don't know. But Josh has good instincts, and they're obviously trying to tell him something."

Lucas pulled out his gun and checked it methodically, automatically. "So. We stick close?"

"Until this is over." Zach looked at the lawyer. "Got your own damned gun?"

Sighing resignedly, Rafferty patted the left side of his jacket, where only another professional would have spotted a very slight bulge. "Right here. And I hope to hell I never have to use it again."

Zach nodded sober agreement, checking his revolver, then replacing it in its shoulder holster while he watched Lucas bring a briefcase from his room and open it on the coffee table. It was jammed with electronic equipment, and Lucas grunted in satisfaction when a brief check showed them all a clear signal on the small screen.

He closed the case and straightened, looking at the other two. "Well, we're all set. Two signals, clear as a bell. If he leaves his car, the transceiver in his shoulder holster will still guide us." Frowning, Lucas added, "What worries me is how *he'll* know where she goes. If he follows her and Travers spots the tail . . ."

Zach's wide shoulders lifted in a shrug. "Nothing we can do about that now, except stick as close as we can. He won't do anything to put her in greater danger, and he knows surveillance methods. Cross your fingers and hope."

Rafferty, following the other two from the suite, reflected silently that they'd probably spend an uncomfortable night outside the penthouse, bored silly.

At least he hoped they would.

It was late in the afternoon when Raven got back to the penthouse, and she turned her tape player on automatically as soon as she was inside. She opened the top drawer of the small table where the player sat, slipping her purse into it and gazing for a moment at the other purse there.

Another one of the habits she'd made obvious

to Leon was the one concerning her purses. She carried a different purse each time she left the penthouse, always getting one out of this drawer whenever Leon was here. The purse she stared at now was one she'd never carried, because it was the one she intended to have at the final confrontation with Leon.

The one containing her gun.

She closed the drawer slowly, sighing. It was only then, distracted with the vague worry, that she realized Josh was there. She turned and saw him as he stepped into the sunken living room, and she crossed to him instantly with a glowing, welcoming smile. In his arms, she lifted her face for his kiss, everything inside her responding in a fiery surge to his touch.

But she stepped back abruptly, her face going still, and swiftly opened his jacket to stare at the gun.

"Better to be prepared," he said quietly. "When we talked, you were bothered by something."

After a moment, Raven nodded. It didn't surprise her that Josh had sensed her disturbance. "Something nebulous. Nothing I can put my finger on." She closed his jacket, smoothing the material absently. "But you shouldn't be wearing a gun. However it ends, you won't be a part of it, Josh."

He was silent.

She stared up at his face, and anxiety knifed coldly through her. Swallowing hard, she said, "You aren't planning on following me?"

The hands on her shoulders tightened, and something restless stirred in his eyes. "No. That would only put you in danger."

Relief swept over her, and she rested her forehead against his chest for a moment. "It's all planned," she murmured. "And the timing is critical. Hagen and Kelsey will be there—" Abruptly, she swore softly and stepped back, staring down at the bracelet on her arm. "Turn off the mike, Kelsey," she commanded firmly.

"Will he?" Josh asked.

"No," Raven answered, still addressing the microphone hidden in her bracelet. "He's a lousy pervert. Kelsey? Turn off the mike!" She knew only too well that it would remain activated.

Josh started to suggest that she put the bracelet in a drawer somewhere, but the shrill summons of the doorbell stopped the words in his throat. He and Raven stared at each other for a moment, then he swiftly retreated to the bedroom.

Raven drew a deep breath and went to answer, forcing her features into an indifferent mask, which nearly cracked when she saw who was there.

"Theodore. Leon isn't here—"

"I know that." Theodore's thin lips were pressed tightly together; clearly, he hadn't forgiven her slap. "He's waiting down in the limo. If you want to see your merchandise, come with me. We're going now."

Her mind raced wildly. "I don't recall inviting you to come along," she said coolly.

"You think Leon would trust a limo driver with something like this, *Miss Anderson*? I'm driving. Are you coming or not?"

"I'll get my purse." She turned from the door and stepped over to the table, reaching into the drawer and pulling out her purse. The one that counted. "I only hope you know where we're going."

Her comment was automatic; she had no hope at all that Theodore would let something slip. But the scorn in her voice must have gotten to him.

"I think I can find my way to Long Beach," he said stiffly.

Raven pulled on sunglasses and went past him out the door, her face impassive. But her mind was still racing. Had Josh heard? And what was it that was still bothering her? She felt that somehow another piece of the puzzle had dropped into her lap if she could only recognize it.

What was different? Out of sync? Leon's restlessness at lunch, his tension. This abrupt trip—was that planned? To shake off any possible pursuit, maybe. But why was Theodore driving? *All* of Leon's people were trustworthy. The limo had taken him to that house where the twins had been so briefly held, hadn't it? With the regular driver, their operative had reported. Why was Theodore driving today?

Raven was tense all the way down in the elevator, but one suspicion vanished when they stood by the limo. Theodore opened the back door and she saw Leon within the car.

"Good afternoon, my dear."

"Leon." She got into the car. So Theodore hadn't planned a trick of his own, she thought. Still, she had learned to profoundly mistrust anomalies; a sudden change in anyone's routine was a danger signal, especially when that routine was as set as Leon's was.

Why was Theodore driving?

"I apologize for giving you no notice, my dear," Leon said smoothly. "I hope you had no plans?"

"None at all." Training held; there was nothing

in her voice to indicate her furiously racing mind. "Frankly, Leon, I'm simply glad that finally we are getting down to business. I could lose an important commission if my clients found their merchandise elsewhere."

"I believe you'll find the merchandise satisfactory," he said indifferently.

Conscious of the extra weight her gun lent the purse in her lap, Raven said, "I gave you a rather long list; not every item is available today?"

"No." Leon stared straight ahead. "But the special item you requested is. Twins."

She infused her voice with cool satisfaction. "Good. The largest commission of all for me."

"I knew you'd be pleased, my dear."

Josh wasted no time in getting to his car. He had told Raven he wouldn't follow her, and he had intended to keep his word, knowing that he would likely be spotted. But he had heard Travers's man say Long Beach, and resolution had vanished.

If he could get there before them, he thought, there was a chance. A small one, but a chance nonetheless. He had to assume they'd take the most direct route to Long Beach, and he had to believe that he would be able to spot them. And if he were careful, he could follow them from that point.

Familiar with the area, he drove swiftly, avoiding heavy traffic and holding himself just below the speed limit; he had no intention of being stopped by a member of the highway patrol. His mind was working, second-guessing Leon Travers and his driver, hoping desperately that his instincts were good.

He had to be there. Had to be as near to Raven as possible when this entire situation reached its final conclusion.

From the beginning there had been little for him to hold on to in all this. Except Raven, and that certainty was still too new and wondrous for him to fully comprehend. As for the rest . . .

He couldn't *control* it. Someone else did. Travers. He controlled it. Or . . . A very small part of his mind concentrated on that mental wavering, questioning it, examining an abrupt and deep uncertainty. Something Stuart had said about Hagen . . . or something Serena had said . . . Raven's "nebulous" uncertainty . . .

What was it?

Hagen and Kelsey moved as close to the secluded house as they dared, crouching behind the cover of overgrown shrubs that had once lined a fence. A small case containing electronic equipment lay open beside Kelsey, and the soft sounds of people talking came from the tiny speaker.

"If you will wait here, my dear, Theodore will get the girls and bring them to you."

Raven's voice, dry and amused: *"Four guards for two teenaged girls? So cautious, Leon. Oh, I'll wait here."* Then, more softly as a door closed in the background: *"If you're leaving the room, Leon, please take these men with you. I'd like to talk to the girls; I don't want them frozen with fear."*

Leon Travers's voice: *"Two of the guards will*

*remain here with you, my dear; I'll take the
others with me. Theodore will remain in here as
well."*

"*Don't you trust me, Leon?*" Raven asked dryly.

"*I trust you, my dear.*"

Hagen was staring at the house and listening
intently to the voices. "Good girl," he murmured.
"We know how many guards, and where at least
two of them will be."

Kelsey's face was stone, and his eyes glittered.
Almost to himself, he muttered, "I should have
known. Dammit, I should have known. After
eight years, why didn't I know? You've lost *two*
agents, you know. Raven. And me."

Hagen sent him a wry look. "I expected as much."

"She's a sitting duck, damn you!" The violence
of Kelsey's voice was softened by need, but not
suppressed. "There are only two of us. How in
hell—"

"More than two," Hagen interrupted dryly, and
gestured slightly.

Kelsey looked, and his bleak face brightened.
"You couldn't have known," he told Hagen flatly.
"There's no way you could have planned this!"

"No appreciation for genius," Hagen murmured
sadly.

Josh reached them then with his three men
behind him. "Hate to crash the party," he said,
words light but tone taut.

"You were expected." Kelsey glared at his boss.
"Apparently."

Hagen spoke before Josh could react to that.
"Mr. Long, you and your men are private citizens
and this is a federal operation," he said in a steely
voice. "You can't—"

"The hell I can't."

Hagen studied the four men, then nodded as if to himself. "Very well. But if you insist on participating in this operation, you must be properly authorized. You work for me or you leave. Now."

Kelsey groaned softly but didn't intrude. And nobody heard his muttered, "That's how he got me."

Josh answered only for himself. "Fine."

Rafferty winced, but answered for himself and the others since they had anticipated this. "Looks like you've got yourself four new—temporary—agents, Hagen."

Hagen nodded in a weighty manner, but his small eyes twinkled brightly for a moment. "Very well. Consider yourselves duly sworn in and authorized agents of the United States government. You answer to me and only me. Armed?"

It was Rafferty who nodded, since Josh was busy listening to the voices still coming from the speaker. "We're armed."

Impatiently, Josh said, "When do we move?"

"We move now. This is what I want you to do . . ."

In a rapid tone and concise words, Hagen explained what was going on inside the house, then told the listening men precisely what they were to do in the coming moments. Precisely.

And it took the combined strength of his men, Zach included, to keep Josh from strangling Hagen then and there.

Just minutes later, while they were waiting much nearer the house for their carefully timed move, Kelsey murmured wistfully to Hagen, "He almost got you."

More shaken than he cared to admit, Hagen

muttered, "A miscalculation on my part. From all reports, Long is extremely cool under pressure."

"Not this kind of pressure. You forgot to figure love into the equation," Kelsey pointed out, enjoying his boss's discomfiture despite everything.

"I always learn from my rare mistakes," Hagen said.

It took all the control she'd mustered over the years for Raven to keep cool when she first saw the girls. So young. So innocent of cruelty until this had happened to them. Like her sister. Like herself. They were identically beautiful, fragile, delicate—and half mad with fear.

Forced to keep her alter ego alive because of Theodore and the watching guards, Raven acted her part. She walked around them as though they were so much cattle on the auction block, subtly maneuvering them until they were standing, shaking and clinging to each other, near one end of a battered love seat; one shove from her and both would be somewhat protected from gunfire behind the furniture.

"Healthy?" she snapped at Theodore.

"Certainly."

"Virgins?" She hated the question, hated watching the girls wince and shrink away from her brutally businesslike tone.

"Doctor's certificate."

"I trust you haven't been drugging them."

"Of course not," Theodore said calmly.

Something moved in the back of Raven's mind, heavy and slow. It was *wrong;* there was something wrong here.

But she played her part. And even while she played her part, her mind was working on several levels.

The major portion of her mind was occupied with thoughts of Josh and their love. She wished she had been able to tell him again that she loved him—just in case. Wished they had shared more time together—just in case. Wished she had told him the dozens of tiny little things that didn't really matter—just in case. Wished that she knew his favorite color . . . his favorite music . . . his favorite food—just in case.

Wished she could touch him.

On another level of her mind were the wispy flashes that were a kind of summing up of things left undone, unsaid, which always filtered through her thoughts at times like this. A lingering curiosity about the three men who seemed so close to Josh. Regret that she had not thanked Kelsey for being a good partner. Faint irritation that she had never told Hagen what she *really* thought of his devious methods and his invariable habit of—

Hagen. Hagen, who never told anyone everything, who always schemed within plots, and then plotted within schemes.

With a silent crash inside her head, everything came together. Her vague uneasiness of today made sense now—at least partially. Seemingly unrelated facts in a history made sense. *That* was what was wrong. A leopard couldn't change its spots. She knew. Suddenly, she knew. Not *why*, because there had to be facts she was unaware of, but *who*.

Hagen, a wily old leopard who would never change, could never change. Leon, a leopard who had changed too quickly, too abruptly.

And Leon wasn't in the room!

Raven felt that everything stopped, and then time advanced in agonizingly slow motion. Her back to Theodore and the guards, she stared at the girls, seeing each nervous blink, each frightened shift of the eyes.

She kept her body easily relaxed with a tremendous effort, but all her consciousness was focused in listening. It would come first in the other room; it had to come first in the other room because—

"Leon didn't mention price," she said without turning.

Flatly, Theodore quoted a price, clearly nonnegotiable.

The sound she heard was only a distant thump, but Raven was reacting. With one hand she shoved the girls violently while her other hand dived into the purse and emerged with a gun. In the same moment, even as shots sounded in the other room, she was dropping behind a chair, her gun rising, aiming unerringly at Theodore.

And the rabbity little office boy was reacting, his thin face twisting in an expression of violent rage, nothing timid or nervous about him now. He clawed for his belt, for the gun she could see at his waist.

In the same instant, one of the guards dived toward the hallway, and Raven was almost instinctively aware that he was met there, crushed in a pair of powerful, merciless arms that belonged to one of Josh's men.

The front door crashed open, and Kelsey was on the floor, his gun pointed at the second, frozen guard.

And behind Theodore, an arm extended to close

about his throat, lifting him literally off his feet. "I wouldn't," Josh said in a very gentle tone, plucking the gun from Theodore's belt.

Into the jarringly silent, frozen tableau walked Hagen very calmly. He stepped over Kelsey, looking only at Theodore, and his smile was a mixture of triumph and cold delight.

The door to the other room opened and Leon stepped out, his arm around a small dark woman with a thin face and haunted eyes, a woman smiling, crying with obvious happiness.

Hagen looked at them for a moment, then returned his gaze to Theodore's livid face. "Theodore Thorpe Thayer the Third," he said, clearly enjoying every syllable, "I hearby arrest you for the crimes of kidnapping, trafficking in human beings . . ."

Nine

"I could kill him!"

Josh laughed a bit ruefully. "I almost did."

They were in the penthouse apartment for a last night—courtesy of a grateful U.S. government Hagen had said, although he hadn't managed to placate anybody with *that* fiction—and were in bed together.

Raven shook her head. She was lying on her stomach beside Josh, and gazing at him as he sat leaning back against the headboard of the bed. "That snake didn't tell me *anything*! I never considered Theodore as a threat, except to my virtue. If I hadn't figured out at least part of it there at the end, he might have shot me before I could react."

Josh was still rueful. "It appears that your esteemed ex-boss had everything neatly worked out. He *knew* you'd guess the truth. He *knew* Zach, Rafferty, Lucas, and I would show up to lend the support he'd need. He *knew* that Travers would somehow manage to get his wife alone, leaving the other two guards ready to be grabbed by us. He *claims* that he even knew exactly how the guards in the living room would react."

Josh shook his head, beyond astonishment, having exhausted his repertoire of curses hours before. "The man's a lunatic."

Almost unwillingly, Raven laughed. "You must admit—he was right on all counts."

Josh toyed with a strand of her long hair, smiling at her. "By the skin of all our teeth—yes!"

"I should have guessed sooner," she said in self-censure. "It was there all along. I'd studied the file on Leon until I could have recited every fact. But it wasn't until I'd spent time with him that I began to wonder why he'd changed so radically, so suddenly. Until three years ago he was not only a law-abiding citizen, but also active in charity work. Then overnight he turned into a particularly evil type of criminal."

Soberly, Josh said, "I'll never stop regretting how badly I misjudged that man. In hell for three years, working as delicately as any surgeon to gather information that would put Thayer away— and all the time knowing that a false move by him would mean his wife's death."

"And then contacting Hagen," Raven agreed, "and knowing what a chance he was taking. Literally putting his wife's life in Hagen's hands. He had the information he needed to get Theodore, but that wouldn't have helped Christine, unless he could somehow be with her when Theodore was grabbed. She was moved from house to house with the girls every time, and Leon never knew where until he took a buyer to see them."

Josh nodded. "It was a smart move on his part to demand that he see her whenever he had to escort buyers to see the girls. And since he'd been doing that for over a year now, Thayer grew less suspicious." He smiled suddenly. "Your maxim: People don't feel threatened by things they're accustomed to."

"At least it worked this time. Leon always went into another room to visit with Christine, and the guards had begun to leave them alone together. It was no problem for Leon to signal your men outside, and after Lucas forced the window . . ."

She was silent for a moment, then shook her head wonderingly. "Poor Leon. He hated white slavery above all else, but he had to stand by for three years with a gun held to his wife's head and watch it happening. It must have torn him apart, seeing those girls."

Softly, Josh said, "I can understand how he must have felt. If someone held a gun to your head, I'd do anything they asked."

Raven caught the hand gently caressing her cheek, holding it against her. "I know."

Josh tried to keep his mind on the conversation. "I've heard of devious plots before, but Thayer is really something. Blowing up that yacht three years ago so that Travers's wife could publicly 'die' and then using Travers and all his money and connections as an elaborate cover for his slavery ring."

"He is related to Leon, you know," Raven said almost absently. "Some kind of fourth cousin or something. He knew how much Leon loved Christine, knew he'd do anything—anything at all—to keep her alive and well." Remembering suddenly, she said, "You told me how *you* managed to get to the house in time, but what about the others?"

"They had me bugged," Josh explained dryly. "Apparently, Zach was certain I'd go chasing after you—I can't imagine why—and he decided they should run along to make sure I didn't hurt myself."

Raven giggled.

Disgusted, Josh said, "Well, that's how it sounded when he explained it to me. Seems they felt I hadn't been myself lately, and that I'd very likely go berserk just any minute." He sighed. "Zach, damn him, had pretty much figured things out, but he didn't feel certain enough to confide in me. That's what he said too—confide."

"Did I hear you rehire all three of them?" Raven asked curiously.

"Well, I'd fired them when they caught up to me at the house. I wasn't happy, you understand. And then they kept me from strangling Hagen, which I didn't consider a blessing. But Zach got that guard, and Rafferty and Lucas took care of the ones in the other room. So I pretty much had to rehire them."

"Of course," she murmured gravely.

He was grave as well, but his lips twitched. "I'm surprised they let me carry a loaded gun," he said aggrievedly.

Raven widened her eyes at him. "And you such a big boy, all grown up and everything."

Josh laughed. "Well, you have to admit they were somewhat overprotective."

"Maybe," she offered solemnly, "they're fond of you."

He laughed again, then reclaimed the earlier subject. "I do have a question. Did Hagen lie about that operative seeing Travers visit the twins once before?"

Raven shook her head. "No, that was the truth. It was just before Leon contacted him. Apparently, another thing Leon insisted on was that he make certain the girls were well treated. So he'd visit them once, try to see they were all right. The chauffeur—who was Theodore's man all the way— never told him where the girls were, he just drove there; and they were always moved immediately afterward.

"But *Theodore* always drove when Leon took buyers, because he wanted to oversee everything. He didn't trust Leon not to try subtly to persuade a buyer *not* to buy. And, since Christine was always there, Theodore wanted to keep an eye on them."

Sighing, Josh murmured, "Hagen knew *that* too."

"He's something, isn't he? And that was partly why I finally realized the truth. The abrupt change in Leon had been worrying me, until I suddenly thought of another maxim—that a leopard can't change its spots. That also applied to Hagen, but in reverse. Leon *shouldn't* have changed the way he apparently did, and Hagen *wouldn't* have changed, which meant he hadn't told me the whole truth.

"Once I realized that, it stood to reason that I had to throw out most of what Hagen had told me, and just rely on what I knew to be truth:

Leon's background. It had to be Theodore. There wasn't anyone else."

"You were quicker than I was," Josh told her. "I knew only that you were bothered, and that something didn't feel right to me. Maybe I was remembering unconsciously that Travers had once been a different man. The only thing I'm sure of is that something both my stepfather and sister told me was ringing alarm bells in my head."

"What was that?"

"That Hagen was devious as hell." Josh laughed. "And when *Serena* says that about someone, it has to be a drastic case!"

Thoughtfully, Raven said, "I can't wait to meet her."

"She can't wait to meet you. Don't be surprised if she refers to you as my Waterloo."

"You said something along those lines once." Raven smiled at him, still holding his hand against her cheek. "If I remember correctly, there seemed to be some question at that point as to whether or not I'd break you."

Suddenly grave, Josh gazed into her eyes, his own warm and tender. "I wondered, then. I was half crazy, scared to death you weren't what I thought." He cleared his throat. "Then when I had to—what did Hagen say?—make a public fool of myself? I knew then that it wouldn't have mattered. If you *had* been what you pretended to be, I would have loved you, wanted you anyway.

"If that means I was broken, then I was. Nothing mattered but you."

Shaken, Raven turned her lips into his palm briefly. "You weren't broken," she said huskily.

"There's so much strength in you. No matter how bad things got, you never gave up on us. You never lost sight of what we meant to each other."

Moving suddenly, Josh slid downward and drew her close, into his arms. "There hasn't been a moment I haven't loved you since the night we met," he told her deeply, brushing a strand of gleaming black hair from her face, his fingers lingering to trace the delicate line of her jaw.

"Josh . . ." She slid her arms around his neck, her lips responding instantly to his.

He lifted his head, smiling. "It feels like years since I've asked you to marry me."

She laughed a little, her breath catching. "I think it has been years!"

He stroked the curve of her breast, his face intent. "I seem to recall that old-fashioned persuasion failed me once. I wonder if it would now. . . ."

Raven caught her breath again, her eyes half-closing as heated pleasure swirled to life within her. "Well, you might try it and find out," she murmured.

His head bent, lips finding her breast in a fiery, seeking touch. "My kingdom needs a princess," he said against her flesh, and the slight vibration of his words sent a shiver through her.

"Oh, yes?"

"My homes a hostess." His hands caressed with slow, sure knowledge.

"Ummm?"

"My bed a mistress." His lips strung a trail of hot kisses over her breasts, up her throat, then teasingly touched her yearning mouth lightly again and again. Then he kissed her hard, deeply, his mouth possessing.

Raven could only gasp when his head lifted, her breath stolen from her.

"And I need a wife." His voice was hoarse now, his eyes darkened and glowing.

Most of her voice had gone with her breath, but Raven tried. "To love and cherish?"

"Forever."

She gazed up at him, her eyes shining, vividly alive and loving. "I think it's working," she said dreamily.

"You haven't said yes," he whispered, kissing her again.

"I haven't heard a question."

His laugh was soft and unsteady. "That's true. Will you marry me, my darling Raven?"

"Yes . . . oh, yes . . . I love you, Josh."

Quite some time later, Josh reached out to turn off the lamp, pulling Raven closer with his other arm. He was roused from impending sleep by a memory before he reached the light. Hesitating, he asked, "Did you tell Hagen you were quitting, darling?"

"He told me." Raven yawned and snuggled closer, warm and pleasantly tired. "And thanked me very politely for being such a good operative all these years."

A little puzzled but not overly concerned, Josh wondered aloud, "Why'd he tell me he'd be in touch, then?"

Raven was still for a moment, then raised herself on an elbow. Her expression was cautious.

"Josh, when you and the others got to the house did Hagen *say* anything?"

"He told us we were private citizens and couldn't be allowed to interfere."

Raven half-closed her eyes. "And?"

"And told us we could either work for him or leave." Josh began to understand her rather odd expression as his words sank in, and he finished somewhat hollowly. "Needless to say, we weren't about to leave. So . . ."

"Josh, tell me he didn't draft you. *Please* tell me he didn't swear you in?"

He cleared his throat and ventured, "It can't be legal. Can it be legal?"

She dropped her forehead against his chest with a moan. "Damn him. I'll kill him. This time, I swear I'll kill him!"

Josh began to laugh. "He just said we were duly authorized and sworn-in agents of the government. It was just a temporary thing, because of the situation."

Raven lifted her head. "That's what *you* think," she said darkly.

There was still, in Josh, a trace of disbelief. "Not even Hagen," he said, "would be that devious. Besides, he didn't look at all happy with me when I tried to strangle him."

She brightened. "Maybe you're safe then. Or maybe not. We'd better take an extended honeymoon far—far—away. Where he won't be able to extradite us."

Josh blinked. "Raven—"

"He's *ruthless*, darling, you just don't know. But if we get away fast enough, he won't have time to whip up this assignment that just *demands* your special talents. With any luck at all, he'll forget about you by the time we come back."

"You're serious," Josh realized.

Raven turned out the light, and her voice reached him thoughtfully in the darkness. "The South Pacific? We could go island-hopping. He wouldn't find us. With any luck *at all*."

"He couldn't have planned it!"

Epilogue

Kelsey was packing away his equipment in the shabby apartment, and sent Hagen a look. "You misjudged Long," he reminded him irritably. "What makes you think you've got the others pegged?"

Hagen contemplated his cigar with a faint smile. "I told you that I always learn from my, er, rare mistakes."

Kelsey snorted. "Right. Well, Raven won't let you get your hands on him anyway."

"True. By the way, my boy, there's a small matter in New Orleans—"

"I'm on vacation," Kelsey snapped.

"I thought you were quitting," Hagen muttered, but didn't push it. "Well, it can wait."

Kelsey gazed at the neatly packed equipment, then looked at Hagen. "Which one of them are you going to shanghai first?"

His boss took no offense at the term, but continued to gaze at his cigar almost dreamily. "Rafferty Lewis. An assignment in the Caribbean which cries out for a man of his special abilities. . . .

THE EDITOR'S CORNER

This summer is going to be one of the best ever! That's not a weather forecast, but a reading report. There will be some very special publishing events you can look forward to that reach just beyond the regular LOVESWEPT fare—which, of course, is as wonderful as always. Alas, I'm limited by space, so I have to try to restrain my urge to describe these books in loving detail. (How I regret that brevity is not one of my virtues!)

During the first week of next month, a brilliant and heartwarming love story will appear in your bookstores—**NEVER LEAVE ME** by Margaret Pemberton. (This Bantam book may be housed in romance sections of some stores, general fiction of others. Do look for it or ask your bookseller to pull a copy for you. Trust me, this is a story you will *not* want to miss!) British, a mother of five, and a wonderfully stylish and talented storyteller, Margaret was first published by us in December 1985. That novel, **GODDESS,** was the compelling love story of Valentina, a mysterious young woman who became a legendary film star, and Vidal, the passionate, powerful, unattainable man who was her discoverer and director. This story often comes hauntingly to my mind. Now, in **NEVER LEAVE ME**, Margaret tells the equally haunting, yet quite different story of Lisette de Valmy, of her forbidden love and a secret that very nearly shatters her happiness. The man she will marry, Greg Derring, is nothing short of marvelous . . . and the climax of the book is so full of emotional richness and poignancy that I dare you to finish the story dry-eyed.

The following month you have an enormous, happy surprise—the zany, chilling, sexy **HOT ICE** by Nora Roberts. I bet you've loved Nora's more than forty romances during the last few years as much as I have. (Yes, we do love books published by our honorable competitors!) How were we so lucky that we got to publish a Nora Roberts book? Well, because what she is writing for us is outside the range of her Silhouette love stories. **HOT ICE** is a romantic suspense, a zesty adventure tale with a grand love story between an ice cream heiress, Whitney, and a criminal—a real, non-garden variety thief with plenty of street smarts—Doug. They're the sassiest, most delightful couple I've encountered since *Romancing The Stone* and the first episode

(continued)

of *Moonlighting*! In the back of **HOT ICE** you'll get an excerpt of Nora's next romantic suspense novel, **SACRED SINS,** an absolutely breathtaking tale, which will be published in December, on sale the first week of November.

THE DELANEY DYNASTY LIVES ON! In July we will distribute a free sampler to tease you unmercifully about the marvelous trilogy **THE DELANEYS OF KILLAROO,** which gives you the love stories of three dynamite ladies of the Australian branch of the Delaney family. But we won't torment you long, because the full works go on sale in early August. Of course these fabulous books were written by the ladies of **THE SHAMROCK TRINITY:** Kay Hooper, Iris Johansen, and Fayrene Preston.

I must rush along now so that, hopefully, I can tantalize you with a few words on the LOVESWEPTs for next month.

NOT A MARRYING MAN by Barbara Boswell, LOVE-SWEPT #194, reintroduces you to a shameless rogue you met briefly before, Sterne Lipton. (Remember him? He's the brother of the heroine of **LANDSLIDE VICTORY.**) Well, Sterne has more than met his match in Brynn Cassidy. When she finds out he's wagered a bundle on getting her into bed, she sets out to teach the ruthless bachelor a ruthless lesson. But soon both of them are wildly, madly, completely in love with one another . . . and in deep hot water. Funny, touching, **NOT A MARRYING MAN** is one more superb love story from Barbara, whose work never fails to delight.

I can't tell you what a pleasure it was for me to work on Sara Orwig's witty and wonderful, **WIND WARNING,** LOVE-SWEPT #195. Savannah Carson and Mike Smith crash into one another on boats in Lake Superior. Mike quite literally falls overboard for the lovely lady, too, but grave danger denies them the freedom to stay together. **WIND WARNING** should carry a cautionary label—its heroine and hero just might steal your heart.

Never, ever has a tent in the wilderness held a more exciting couple than in Hertha Schulze's **SOLID GOLD PROSPECT,** LOVESWEPT #196. Heroine Nita Holiday is a woman with whom each of us can readily identify as we learned so well in Hertha's first LOVESWEPT, **BEFORE AND AFTER,** because she's an avid romance reader. Mr. Right seems to her to have stepped right off the page of a LOVESWEPT when she sets eyes on Matt Lamartine. And

(continued)

Matt can scarcely tear himself away from the beguiling woman whose background is so different from his own that it shakes him right down to his toes. From New York to Chicago to the vast, romantic wilderness of Canada, Nita and Matt pursue passion . . . and the understanding that can make their love last forever. An utterly sensational romance.

As the New Year began some months ago I was thinking back over the years, remembering the writers with whom I've had long relationships. Among them, of course, is Sandra Brown whose warm friendship I have enjoyed as much as her superb professionalism. One of the many things I admire about Sandra is that she never rests on her laurels. She constantly challenges herself to achieve new writing goals—and all of us are the beneficiaries. In her next romance, **DEMON RUMM**, LOVESWEPT #197, you'll see another instance of how Sandra continues to expand her mastery of her craft for she writes this story exclusively from the hero's point-of-view. Rylan North is a famous, enigmatic, perfectionistic movie idol. Tapped to star as Demon Rumm, the late husband of the heroine, Kirsten, he moves into her house . . . her life . . . her very soul. Sultry and sensitive, this romance is one of Sandra's most memorable. A true keeper.

We hope you will be as excited as we are over the line-up of LOVESWEPTs and other novels that we've developed for a sensational summer of reading.

With every good wish,

Carolyn Nichols

Carolyn Nichols
  Editor
LOVESWEPT
Bantam Books, Inc.
666 Fifth Avenue
New York, NY 10103

LOVESWEPT

Love Stories you'll never forget by authors you'll always remember

☐	21792	**Too Many Husbands #159** Charlotte Hughes	$2.50
☐	21782	**Bedside Manners #160** Barbara Boswell	$2.50
☐	21784	**Seeing Stars #161** Fran Baker	$2.50
☐	21785	**Secrets of Autumn #162** Joan Elliot Pickart	$2.50
☐	21781	**Still Waters #163** Kathleen Creighton	$2.50
☐	21799	**Whatever It Takes #164** Barbara Boswell	$2.50
☐	21800	**Kevin's Story #165** Adrienne Staff & Sally Goldenbaum	$2.50
☐	21774	**Listen For The Drummer #166** Joan Elliott Pickart	$2.50
☐	21791	**Scamp Of Saltillo #170** Peggy Webb	$2.50
☐	21772	**Finnegan's Hideaway #171** Sara Orwig	$2.50
☐	21764	**Inherited #172** Marianne Shock	$2.50
☐	21780	**Emerald Fire #173** Nancy Holder	$2.50
☐	21795	**Where The Heart Is #174** Eugenia Riley	$2.50
☐	21796	**Expose #175** Kimberli Wagner	$2.50
☐	21794	**'Til The End Of Time #176** Iris Johansen	$2.50
☐	21802	**Hard Habit To Break #177** Linda Cajio	$2.50
☐	21807	**Disturbing The Peace #178** Peggy Webb	$2.50
☐	21801	**Kaleidoscope #179** Joan Elliott Pickart	$2.50
☐	21797	**The Dragon Slayer #180** Patt Bucheister	$2.50
☐	21790	**Robin And Her Merry People #181** Fayrene Preston	$2.50

Prices and availability subject to change without notice.

Buy them at your local bookstore or use this handy coupon for ordering: